I0817853

THE CYCLIST

The Cyclist

A Love Story for the Ages

A. W. STRIPLING, JR.

Publishing Futures

Contents

Dedication

To Noah, Daisy, Bell, and Gracey
and my other loving family members

In the Country

Since the time of Aristotle, political philosophers have noted that those who live in cities have a different sensibility than those who live in the countryside. As suburbs continued to citify and exurbs died, the difference between the two became more pronounced.

A Bible and a Korean War Veteran baseball cap sat on the dashboard of a pickup truck parked along the Main Street business district. Dan Cooper walked inside Cordelia's only diner that served a full breakfast at 6 AM every day of the week. A few booths were full and only two seats at the counter were still empty. Dan said hi to Thomas and James who were deep in discussion about Friday night's high school football game. He walked to the booth at the end of the counter and joined his three friends who were also deep in conversation. The "breakfast club" met for senior coffees and breakfast every morning like clockwork. It was how they had started the day since their wives had passed away or run away or gotten too sick to cook and keep house any longer. Dan arrived in the middle of a serious debate about whether the peaches were going to do well this season. This year, fruit growers are experiencing one of the warmest winters in more than 60 years. Most deciduous fruit trees, such as peach trees, adapt to winter cold and require a certain number of chill hours to produce a good harvest. As of Feb. 1, the Chilton Research and Extension Center in Clanton, Alabama, has logged 587 hours between 32 and 45° F. This is much less than the 10-year average of 799 hours, and the 59 year average of 997 hours. By seven, the diner was nearly empty. Until lunchtime, its only visitors would be the occasional trucker stopping on his way into or out of the nearby city. Occasionally a car full of city people on their way to another city stopped in to mingle with the "country folk" for a day. It was a form of entertainment for them.

City people did not see the people of the outer parts as equals. City people have a fundamentally different approach to life from their country counterparts. They have high expectations for their lifestyle: the power doesn't go out, the water is hot in moments, the mail comes every day, and the supermarket is full of food that is fresh and exotic. City people work, usually very hard in often humiliating jobs to pay for a tiny apartment, a high car payment, and those luxuries they've grown used to. For the lucky ones who can still travel in this post-energy-rich era - who have a view of the country at all - it is from a 75 mph window on the way to somewhere more scenic.

City people want it all now, and they don't want excuses about why they should have to wait. The city is a very competitive place. It seldom occurred to them that the people in these country communities supplied them with most of the things they need.

Chapter 1

In the City

In the city, there is the hustle and bustle day and night. Some need the light, then some feed off the darkness of the night. Some run to keep in shape. Some never leave the confines of their shelter. Some do not have shelter. Some enjoy food while others go hungry. Cities, including this one, are a combination of the grand and seedy. The rich get richer while the poor grow more miserable, but the middle never changes. The teachers teach children while the seniors visit their recreation centers. They revisit old times and are still trying to get a little piece of the action that the city gives back. There are writers, bakers, taxicab drivers, police officers, and movie stars all giving back to the metropolis they love. The writers write daily while the bakers bake twice daily to feed all its inhabitants. The taxi driver ferries all the people around while the policemen watch over them. There are sports teams with billions on the payroll; football, baseball, soccer, and the basket one too. Then there are kids on the street playing the same games for no pay at all.

Deep in the heart of the city lies the entertainment district; the parties roll on until the break of dawn. South metro is where most of the businesses are, snooty and wealthy, putting the poor man down. Uptown is where most of the middle live. They fancy their neighborhood, those uptowners do. To the east and west lie the roads that feed the metropolis its eggs, meat, and milk, those very harvests that the people of the metropolis take for granted but consume every hour.

Every once and a while, the country folk come to play in the city for a day or even for a weekend downtown and occasionally uptowners go downtown. They come with their money and a chance of luck. Downtown is where the seedy city lies with its gamblers, thieves, and prostitutes. roaming with the has-beens and the who knows. The policemen hardly venture to the streets of downtown except for the times they are collecting their dirty money when no one else is around. Some churches line the streets of this city, twenty-four-hour confessional booths, priests that have dedicated their lives to rid the masses of their sins. Friday, Saturday, Sunday, you pick your Sabbath, but unlike some cities, in New Atlanta Metropolis, the religions do not fight or quarrel. The different faiths seem to accept one another and mingle easily with those who are atheists or agnostics.

Meanwhile, the outer district is where all of the crops grow, and the tales are tall. In the years after the pandemics, the country folk became ever more isolated from those living in the cities. One such inhabitant of these outer farm communities is what you might call a dreamer, always looking off to the next sunset, not the one at hand. James, a first-generation countryman, brought his family out of the city when the first plague began. Nine years have passed since the second great depression started. Most people, whether city and country, think it will never really end.

James is finishing his coffee and conversation and about to head to the field to oversee his farm helpers. He thinks about Anne, who is at home taking care of Liza, their two-year-old daughter. She had helpers as well. Murphy, their dog, and three cats named Squirt, Andy, and Cyrus all lived in their farmhouse. It was your typical old farmhouse, whitewashed wood with a wrap-around porch, and a large oak tree planted in Anne's name when they started their new lives there. James was happy with his life, content to grow the fruits and vegetables that graced the tables in the city. Times had grown hard for the small family farmers with fewer restaurants and businesses in the cities that bought fresh foods. James, however, still dreamed of the life he wanted when he moved to the outer regions, and to complete that picture, he longed for a son. He and Anne were sure that if they had a second child, it would be a boy. This morning, Ann had been sick, as she had been when she carried Liza. After a few months of disappointment, she told James that he was about to be a father again.

As soon as the dream became his reality, James was worried that times might not get easier and he was not sure that he would be able to watch his son grow up on their family farm. He needed a plan that would offer his son a life that was not as uncertain and challenging as the one he and Anne were living. James came up with a plan for his unborn son.

The winter came and went, and Anne's pregnancy was going well. Anne felt radiant and assured James that it would be a boy. She said she could tell by how low he sat in her womb. The baby was due to be born in July. Spring rolled through as James worked on the farm, preparing his crop for sale in the city farmers markets and schools. Anne enjoyed tea on the front porch each morning, dreaming of what her son's life would be with them. Anne was not privy to James' ultimate plan for the boy. She only dreamed of what she might want for him.

May came and went as well as June and July. One morning, Anne went into labor. James grabbed her bag and put it in the car, and they headed for the hospital. Now, this was the only hospital for a hundred miles, and Anne had been there nearly three years ago. Much to Anne's chagrin, when she finally reached the hospital, she was almost fully dilated. They placed her in the delivery room, and the midwife began her duties. Anne looked up and saw a familiar crack in the ceiling and remembered that she had been in that very room when Liza was born. Suddenly, she also remembered the pain of that delivery and was afraid. James stood outside the delivery room, waiting nervously. One hour went by. Two hours went by with no news from the delivery room. Finally, around five p.m., the midwife emerged from the delivery room. "Mr. Liden," she said, "you have a beautiful baby boy." James was elated, and the celebration began. He rushed to his wife's side in the recovery room, and he felt her exhaustion, but she had done the single greatest thing for James by giving him a beautiful son, and he was grateful. He loved her at that moment more than he believed possible.

In two days, they brought the baby home, and the time just seemed to fly by for the young couple. The baby was healthy, the crops were fruitful, and James continued to work on his secret plans. He loved the boy. The first year went by, and then the second, the boy learned to talk, and everyone in the small farming community loved him. His third birthday came and went, and the boy was growing strong. Anne loved being the mother of her two children, and she would dream of the day they married and had children of their own. They would take over the work of the house and the farm and would take care of Anne and James in their old age. That was the life of a country family.

James knew in a short while the boy would have to start school, and the country was no place for him. James had been putting some money aside over the last few years, always keeping his plan to himself. Anne knew deep in her heart that James wanted more for the boy than to be a farmer from the country but she loved their lives and did not understand his concerns. His fourth birthday and then his fifth in July passed. James knew he would have to start school that following year. The boy and his father played endless games of catch in the front of the house, just near the cornfields that summer. The time for implementing his plan for his son was drawing near. The year rolled around until his sixth birthday. July turned to August, and the days were hard for James. The last week of August came. The sunset and rose, but the Sunday of that week came. James told Anne he was taking a ride to get feed, and he would be back later; Gabriel was going with him. Anne was confused but not suspicious. The boy's father had packed some clothes the day before for the boy in a suitcase, he grabbed it, and they began the slow trip down the dirt road. They passed the intersection that led to the feed store and continued toward the larger highway that led to the city. The boy asked where they were going? He said, "The feed store is down the other road," his father did not answer. The boy kept asking, "Where are we going?"

His father would reply the same way every time, "Gabriel, it's for your own good."

They continued in the truck for two and a half hours had passed, and the boy saw a sign on the road that said the city limits were only twenty-five miles. The boy began to get scared. The boy said to his father, "I thought our kind didn't go to the city."

His father just replied, "Sometimes we go there This is for your own good."

They entered the toll booth, "Toll please," said the toll booth operator. James handed her the money, and they drove through the gate into the metropolis, cars flying by at great speeds. James made a signal to get off the highway and onto a surface street, the boy, now near panic, asked his father, "Where are we going? Where are you taking me?"

Over and over, James replied, "It's for your own good."

They continued down the street; James was pensive. Gabriel was scared and feeling uncertain. Anne was unaware of the events taking place. They were in the downtown district, the streets lined with homeless people pushing grocery carts and groups of people hanging out on the sidewalk, smoking, and looking disinterested. His father was staying his course. They drove to one hundred and thirty-fourth street and made a right into a fenced compound. James drove up to a call box, and a voice answered.

"Highland Boys School," came from the box.

The boy shouted, "Father, no! What have I done?"

"It's for your own good," said James with tears in his eyes. "I'm here with Gabriel Liden. This is James Liden."

"Good afternoon Mr. Liden. Proceed through the gates to the fourth building on the right. The headmaster will greet you at the entrance to the building," politely said the voice from the box.

"Oh, okay, thank you," said James putting the truck in gear and starting to pull forward.

His father drove slowly, wondering if he was doing the right thing. He knew his son needed a better life, and the city was the only way to get it. I will just drop the boy and leave, that is what is best, he thought. I cannot show emotion. The boy must be scared.

Gabriel was in the passenger seat of the truck crying slow tears in agony. He didn't know what he had done. They passed a tennis court, and the boy didn't know what it was. The Liden's couldn't afford a television, so Gabriel didn't know of such sports. After the second great depression started, things like electronics became scarce; the global supply chain was interrupted a couple of decades before and never really recovered. Commoners like the Liden's just couldn't get such exotic things as televisions. They passed the third building on the right, and Gabriel, now with a running nose and tear-stained cheeks, pleaded with his father, begging him to take him home. They rounded the corner. The boy could see a man standing at the entrance to the fourth building. He looked stern. He was dressed in a grey suit and a black hat and stood steady and unwavering. James parked the car and got out the driver's side door. The boy locked the passenger side and began wailing,

"No, I won't go," cried the boy.

"Gabriel, don't make this harder than it has to be. It is for your own good," yelled James through the window. "You'll understand someday."

The headmaster was not a tolerant or patient man. He made his way to the truck and said, "Young man, I am a busy man, and I don't have time for your childish antics. Now open that door this instant."

The boy resisted at first, still crying, confused and heartbroken, but soon he gave way. He unlocked the door and stepped out of the passenger side. James went to the truck and grabbed his bag, trying to hold back his tears. He thought to himself; surely this could be easier on the both of us. The headmaster stepped forward and in a low angry voice said, “Tell me your name, boy!”

Gabriel stunned, and in a quivering voice, said, “I am Gabriel Liden and I am six years old.”

“I did not ask your age boy. Don’t you think I know your age?”

Gabriel still didn’t understand what was going on. “Answer me, Gabriel! Don’t you think I know your age?”

“Yes,” said Gabriel, tears still running down his cheek. “But why am I here, father?”

“Gabriel, it's for your own good,” cried his father, tears welling in his eyes.

The headmaster straightened his posture and ran his hands down the front of his dress jacket, “Perhaps I should answer this one, Mr. Gabriel Liden,” said the headmaster. “Your father wants a better life for you. He is convinced that the metropolis is the only way to get that for you. Do you agree with him?”

“No, I don’t. Father, I want to go home, please,” Gabriel said repeatedly and he looked to his father for help. Any sign of compassion would have been welcome, but his father stood there, cold and unwavering, as the headmaster began to address him again.

“This is your home now. Your father has arranged it to be so. There is no changing his or my mind for that matter. Gabriel, you will learn how to be a man here. I will teach you that whether you want me to or not. James, do you have anything to say to your son?”

James went down to his knees so he was looking into Gabriel's eyes. “Gabriel, I know you don’t understand now, but believe me when I say that this is for your own good. You’ll have a better life here, a better future.” James saw the look of betrayal in his son's eyes and fought to maintain eye contact. He failed and rose to his feet.

"What about mom, does she know about this," cried Gabriel looking up at his father?

"Your mother will understand, son. These people can give you a life I could never even begin to imagine for you. Your mother will understand. She has to," said James.

"So, mom doesn't know... I hate you! I hate you," cried Gabriel!

The headmaster motioned to a man lurking in the breezeway. "Mr. Anderson! Come take the boy to his room and introduce him to his new roommate. Come, and make it quick. I need to talk to Mr. Liden alone."

"Yes, headmaster. Come with me, Gabriel," said Mr. Anderson, an average-sized man, dressed in a sharp black suit and red silk tie, pointing the boy towards a door in the breezeway.

"I hate you, father. I never want to see you again. How could you do this to me?"

"Now, now young Liden," said the headmaster, "Hate is a strong word. We will teach you not to use such words in haste here. Run along. There is business to attend to."

"I love you, Gabriel. I promise this is for your own good," exclaimed James.

The boy was hurried off by Mr. Anderson, a counselor at the Highland Boys School in the metropolis. The boy looked back a few times, fighting his anger all the while, wishing he had a chance to talk to his mother once again. The boy was conflicted. His father wanted better for him, but wasn't he better by his father's side? Perhaps his father knew best, but it didn't make it any easier for the boy. The headmaster turned to James and in a deceivingly calm voice said, "They all start this way. He'll come around, don't you worry now. Mr. Liden, there is the matter of payment for the boy's school. You have arranged to pay the first year in full, and the following years you wish to barter for the boy's education, am I right?"

James reached in his old overalls and pulled out an envelope full of cash. "I have the first year in full. My crops will easily pay for his room and board for the years to come. Here, you can count it."

"Cash, how crude. We usually don't accept such payment, Mr. Liden, but you are from the outer parts; we'll just say you didn't know any better," said the headmaster, putting the money in the inside pocket of his suit.

James turned his eyes away and looked down in shame, "When do I get to see him again," asked James nervously?

"We go year-round around here, Mr. Liden. There is very little room for unsupervised visits."

"Surely, you will let me see him often. I will start my deliveries monthly this time next year. I will see him then, right? But surely I will get to see him a few times this year?"

"Mr. Liden, the boy has been in the outer parts for six years. We don't know how much damage has been done to his psyche. You must understand. If you wish him to be of the metropolis, he must not have contact with the outer parts often. He will be in quarantine for a year, and then if he wishes to see you, he will ask to do so."

"But that is not what we bargained headmaster. I love the boy. I am doing what is best for him, but I thought I would still be there for him," asked James fiddling with his keys in his hands, jingling in his old, withered hands.

"Mr. Liden, the reputation of my school could be on the line if word gets out that I am letting the lesser people of the outer parts into my institution. You must see that."

"We are not lesser people, headmaster. We just do things differently. For instance, you couldn't tell me what kind of soil I'd need to grow different crops or how to fix a combined-tractor," James spoke with the true pride of his knowledge of machine and earth. He was not ashamed of his life. He just wanted "more" for Gabriel.

"Mr. Liden, these are things I could easily look up with our vast library, but why would I concern myself with such things; I am from the metropolis. I suggest you go and tend to your crops for they had better be of top quality to feed our young minds next year, your boy included in those minds. The boy is already far behind. I fear we are wasting our time quarreling over small things. So, Mr. Liden, go back to where you belong; do what it is you do best and leave the boy to me."

"Yes headmaster, but I will see him next year, you have my word."

"Yes, Yes, Mr. Liden. I'll expect delivery of the first crops this very day next year. Now I bid you good afternoon, Mr. Liden. Please be on your way."

"Yes, headmaster," said James in a defeated voice. He wanted better for the boy, but was the cost too high, he thought? The headmaster turned and began a self-satisfied stroll towards the breezeway. James, with a churning stomach, turned and got into his vehicle, started the engine, and proceeded back down the cobblestone driveway. He turned and looked. The headmaster gave a slight condescending touch to his hat, and James drove away. He must not look back, he cried. It is for the boy's own good. Forgive me, Anne...

Chapter 2

On Your Own

As his father drove away, Gabriel was escorted to his room in the west wing of Willowbend Hall by Mr. Anderson. He tried to console the boy, let him know his father was doing these things for the very best of reasons. He would have a better life at the Highland Boys School. However, Gabriel, still in shock, began to panic. "What did I do," he thought as slow tears streamed from his eyes down his youthful face.

"Now, now Gabriel, stop those tears," said Mr. Anderson in a calm and tender voice.

"Why would he put me here," cried Gabriel. "Surely, my life is better by his side."

Mr. Anderson placed his hand on Gabriel's shoulder and said, "Gabriel, there are things in the metropolis that you could never find in the outer parts; we understand things differently. We have better lives."

"I had a fine life. My mother loved me. My sister loved me. I thought my father loved me. I'll never get to see Liza or Murphy again. Please tell me this is a dream." Gabriel placed his hands together pulling them to his mouth and slowly walked forward.

"I would love to tell you this is a dream, but it is not."

"No, that's not what I meant. I meant tell me today is just a dream."

Gabriel and Mr. Anderson continued down the hall to the stairs. "Gabriel, I wish you could understand the opportunity that your father is giving you. You will start school here at the Boys School and learn to live a prosperous and comfortable life. All the boys from the Highland Boys School attend the finest universities in metropolises all over the world. You would have never received a proper education in the outer parts."

Mr. Anderson and Gabriel reached the second floor, exited to the right and down the hall toward the fourth door on the left."

"I hate him," said Gabriel. "I wish I was never born."

"Gabriel, you will learn to love it here. You will forget about the outer parts. You may hate your father now, but you will thank him later. Here we are, Gabriel, the fourth room on the left. Here, take your bag and walk in strong like a man."

Gabriel clutched his old and raggedy suitcase and entered his room. It was a sizeable room with a large bay window overlooking the natatorium and a large oak tree surrounded by many smaller maples. There were two beds and two dressers, one already occupied. Mr. Anderson said, "Your roommate should be here any moment. He's probably just using the restroom."

A few moments passed, and Gabriel heard a jubilant whistling from down the hall. His stomach began to churn. "What if he doesn't like me," thought Gabriel, still clutching his old suitcase. Mr. Anderson instructed the boy to look alive; first impressions are always the most important. Gabriel placed the old suitcase on the floor and turned towards the door. The whistle got louder. Mr. Anderson explained to the boy that he probably should not mention the outer parts; it would be in his best interests. The melodic whistle of this unknown person ceased just as he saw a young man come around the corner into that very fourth door on the left. The young man had a well-defined sharp face and brown hair parted to the side and slicked back. He was dressed very well for such a young man, and he stood tall for his age.

"Oh, hello Mr. Anderson! How are you," inquired the young man?

"I'm doing just fine, son. And yourself?"

"Why I couldn't be better, I seem to have the greatest of whistles about me today. It's going to be a good year. Oh, wait! Who's this? Hello there. Are you my new roommate," asked the boy?

"Allow me to do the introductions," said Mr. Anderson. "Gabriel Liden, may I introduce you to Arthur Highland, as in the Highland Boys School."

"Pleasure to meet you, Mr. Liden! Actually, Mr. Gabriel Liden, most people call me Artie, Arthur seems so proper. After all, I'm only seven.."

The two boys exchanged handshakes and Gabriel said sheepishly, "Your parents own this place?"

Artie snickered just a little bit and said, "Well... not really. The school was founded by my family, yes. Now it is run by trustees; my father is on the board."

Gabriel began to look a little uncomfortable as Mr. Anderson started to make his way to the door.

"Where are you going Mr. Anderson," asked Gabriel?

"The first year, every boy is mentored by a student who is older than he is. We thought Arthur would be a wonderful pick for you, Gabriel. He's good with people, and he knows people too," said Mr. Anderson as he gave a wave goodbye. "You'll be fine Gabriel."

"I've never had a roommate, Artie, if I may call you Artie, sir."

"Why are you siring me, Gabriel? I'm here to be your friend and mentor. You can call me Artie Bombgardner if you wish."

Gabriel looking slightly confused asked, "Why would I call you Artie Bombgardner? I thought your last name was Highland."

Authur with a little smirk on his face said, "It is silly; I was making a joke. Gabriel, may I call you Gabe, it seems to fit you."

"I don't see why not, Mr. Bombgardner."

Arthur just laughed as he looked at Gabriel and said, "Funny, there's a little wit in you yet. Now you're getting in the spirit of things. Let's get you unpacked, Gabe."

Mr. Anderson walked out the door and on his way to his office, leaving the two boys to get acquainted. Gabriel was still angry at his father. He began to bury his slight outer accent and tried to forge onward nonetheless. For a moment, the positive antics of his new roommate made him feel just a little at home. He felt like he had found a friend on a day where he thought there was no hope. Artie and Gabriel unpacked his clothing and toiletries. Although Gabriel was guarding the hatred of his father that grew deeper by the moment, he began to realize this day was, in fact, very real and he might as well make the best of it.

"You seem a little quiet, Gabe. What's wrong?" asked Arthur, turning towards him.

"I don't know if I'm going to fit in like the other boys," said Gabriel looking as if he knew he was different.

"Nonsense Gabe, you'll fit like marmalade and bread."

"I'm not from here, Artie."

"I know."

"No, I don't think you do. Mr. Anderson told me not to mention this, but I'm from the..."

"From the outer parts, yes, I know. Remember, my father is on the board of trustees. The reason you are with me, Gabe, is because they know I will keep the secret. Your secret is safe with me, Gabe. Your father is the farmer they contracted,. Anyway, I saw you drive up today. Gabe, in a way, I'm kind of an outcast too. Don't you think people look at me differently because I'm a Highland?"

Gabriel's demeanor eased up as Arthur opened up to him. "I never thought of it that way. But why did my father do this to me? I don't understand."

Arthur thought for a moment. He put down the article of clothing he was folding and said, "Let me guess; you hate your father right now, huh? Well, Gabe, do you think I wanted to come here? I wanted to go to an uptown school. I wanted to live just like real people do. So, in a way, Gabe I hated my father just as bad this same time last year when he told me I wasn't going to an uptown school. I don't want to be downtown necessarily. Downtown isn't what it was some time ago. It's still the best school in the metropolis, but I want to see the nice part of town too, not just this old place. Do you understand, Gabe?"

Gabriel took the last piece of clothing from the suitcase, folded it, and placed it in the drawer. "I guess what you're saying is we're kind of alike, but at the opposite extremes."

"Exactly! Gabe, moving on. We have plenty of time to talk about these things. We're roomies now, but it's lunchtime, and I'm starving, so you wanna go or what?"Arthur leaned up against the wall and pointed towards the open doorway jokingly flexing his arm muscle.

Gabriel smiled at the comic relief and said, "Please, I could use some food."

Arthur and Gabriel made their way across campus to the dining hall. Gabriel felt better now knowing that he was safe from the atrocities of youth: the teasing, the name-calling, and the whatnot so many have known. Their lunch was a luxurious affair for Gabriel, for he had never known such things as braised pork tenderloin or even tenderloin for that matter.

He savored the meal like it was the best he had ever had. He learned at that meal that perhaps there were things he would have and could learn there that his father could not give him or teach him. However, it did not rest his soul and his lack of understanding when it came to his father's decision. The two boys laughed, both as outcasts, sitting alone at a table in the dining hall guffawing and scoffing at the other outcasts. They were all nestled in their little pods of safety.

Arthur explained to Gabriel that there were many secrets in the school called Highland. The greatest he noted was that the unwavering intolerant headmaster he met was, in fact, a gay man who lived in the midtown district, often searching out the seedy life of the downtown district, at least that what his father said. The midtown district was home to the wealthy, the mega-wealthy. They were people like the Highlands and most of the parents of the Highland Boys School students. Don't get me wrong some uptowners attended the school, scholars, and athletes, but most came from the posh midtown district.

Arthur asked Gabriel whether he was interested in sports. The Highland Boys School had the best sports programs in the metropolis. Gabriel told his new friend Arthur that he wasn't familiar with all the sports, but he and his father used to play catch by the cornfields. Arthur laughed at Gabriel, not out of mal intent, but that he couldn't picture cornfields; it seemed so rural. Gabriel took a little offense to his laughter, but Arthur being very intuitive, apologized. Arthur began asking Gabriel about the outer parts; he was very interested. Gabriel told of a great storm rolling in over the massive fields and crops, and days when he and his mother would play hide and seek in the tobacco fields; they always had a wonderful time together. Gabriel began to lament; he missed his mother. He wanted to talk to her, tell her he loved her and that he wanted to be by her side. Gabriel had a feeling he wouldn't get that opportunity any time soon.

They finished their lunch and made it back to the dorms. They talked for a while about the metropolis, eventually had dinner, and made their way to their respective beds for the night. Arthur told him classes would begin tomorrow, and that they would be in separate classes except for physical education. Arthur said he should not tell the others where he was born. He told him to tell the others his father was a businessman, and he was on an academic scholarship from uptown. They wouldn't question that. He asked why he should live a lie as such. Arthur merely explained it would be for the best. He would have a much better time among the harsh youth of the school. Gabriel agreed and said his prayers and went to sleep.

Gabriel did not sleep very well that night, tossing and turning with a knot in his stomach. He often looked over at Arthur, wondering why he was so pleasant to him. That morning he watched the sun crest the horizon through the great oak, shook off the nervousness, and made his way to the showers. He was hoping to get to the bathroom before the other boys. He had never showered in community showers before; he was a little shy. He was showered and ready for class before Arthur had awoken. The clock in the room struck eight-fifteen, and Arthur awoke, sat up, and turned off the alarm; classes began at nine. Arthur said, "You're up early. Guess you didn't sleep too well, huh?"

Gabriel with wet hair and a slight yawn replied, "I slept okay, well actually, I didn't."

"That's okay, Gabe I didn't sleep well my first night either," said Arthur making it out of bed and to the window to see what the day's weather may hold.

"I was a little nervous earlier," said Gabriel. "I don't know how I'm going to do in school. I've never even been out of the outer parts."

Arthur looked rather coy and turned towards Gabriel, "There's one thing I'm sure about Gabe, and that's that you're a smart cookie. Your father had big plans, and maybe he was a smart man, maybe he knew how smart you were."

"I don't want to think about my father ever again, Artie. I still don't understand why he did this to me," said Gabriel with an obvious look of discontent.

"Give it some time, Gabe," said Arthur. "You'll learn to appreciate this place and remember, ever is a very definitive word. Now enough of this! I've got to get to the showers. It's already eight-twenty. You're going to make us late on the first day, and we can't have that, can we?"

"I guess not," said Gabriel sitting in the chair by the window, watching the sunrise on his first day in the metropolis.

Arthur made his way to the showers, washed, and brushed his teeth. He readied himself in under twenty minutes, grabbing Gabriel and running for the auditorium. The two boys ran frantically down the cobblestone driveway, half out of breath until they reached their destination. They opened the double doors to the Chase Auditorium and gymnasium, and Gabriel felt a little overwhelmed. There were elementary, middle, and high school students, all awaiting the first address of the beloved headmaster. Arthur and Gabriel took a seat among the top bleachers, with satchels and class schedules in hand. The headmaster made his way into the podium and readied the mass of students for the address.

"Now students, settle down, settle down. Will everyone, please take their seats," said the headmaster. "Today, we embark on another wonderful school year at the Highland Boys School."

The children clapped, some even whistled. Gabriel was stricken with silence. Arthur reached over and gave Gabriel a slight nudge and a wink like he knew what was coming. Arthur began to mouth at the same time as the headmaster. "All over the world live the graduates of this fine institution," said the headmaster. Gabriel laughed, and his demeanor lightened, appreciating the comic relief his friend had given him. The headmaster went on for about thirty minutes about how this would be the best year that the school had ever seen. Sports! Academics! It was all theirs for the taking. He closed with a famous passage from an alumnus from fifty years ago; "Hoorah for the school of schools," is all the headmaster meant.

Arthur turned to Gabriel and said, "Gabe, let me see your class schedule." Gabriel reached in his satchel that Arthur let him borrow and grabbed his class schedule and gave it to Arthur.

"Let me see here Gabe, looks like you have a socialization class with Mr. Riley first period. Next to physical education with me at eleven just before lunch. Classes start at nine, so I'll have time to show you where Mr. Riley's class is. Any questions?"

Gabriel raised his eyebrows and looked as if he was a little puzzled once again. "What's socialization class, Artie?"

"Socialization class is a one on one session you'll go to each day of classes for the first year of school. It just brings you up to speed, teaches you about the metropolis, and well, some other ones too."

"Very well then," said Gabriel. "I'll try to make the best of it."

"Alright, Gabe. You ready to start this new life of yours?"

"I don't think I have a choice, do I," asked Gabriel?

"Nope, I guess not," said Arthur. "We can skip the last few minutes of this grand old hoorah. Come on, and we'll sneak out the back door."

The boys quietly made their way down the bleachers avoiding eye contact with the headmaster. The headmaster went to showcase something on the wall, and the boys made their escape. They left through the back of the auditorium, Arthur leading Gabriel to safety and in the direction of Mr. Riley's office. Down the cobblestone streets of the school, they went;

Gabriel began to forget about his father. Arthur was becoming the best friend he would ever know.

The time was now nine fifty, and the boys reached Mr. Riley's office. Arthur told Gabriel that it was now time to let go of his past, look to the future, his future at the Highland Boys School. "I must go now, Gabe," said Arthur, "but you'll do just fine. We'll teach you how to live and be Gabe. You'll be a gentleman, don't you worry. See you in an hour or so." Arthur left Gabriel outside of the office and headed out towards his first class.

"Bye," said Gabriel.

He walked down the hall, and his throat seemed to be tightening. He was met by a secretary who greeted him and told him to have a seat. He sat nervously, very nervously until an older bearded man emerged from the adjacent door. "Hello there, son! You must be Gabriel Liden," said the man.

"You must be Mr. Riley, or at least I hope you're Mr. Riley," said Gabriel standing to his feet.

"Indeed, I am Mr. Riley, come on in."

Gabriel walked through the threshold of the door and saw clipping after clipping of newspaper articles, all of them about former students. Mr. Riley sat the boy down in the chair in front of the desk. He asked him if he'd like anything. The boy asked for a glass of water, and the session began.

"Gabriel, let me tell you a little bit about myself and why you're with me today," said Mr. Riley leaning over his large calendar on top of his weathered antique wooden desk. "Did you know that I'm an alumnus of this very fine institution?"

"No, I didn't know, sir," said Gabriel fidgeting in his seat.

"Please don't call me sir it makes me feel old," said Mr. Riley. "Would you like to call me by my first name? Will it make you feel more comfortable?"

"I guess, sir," said Gabriel now trying to sit upright.

"There you go again, son. Just call me Fineous, Fineous Riley."

"Yes, Fineous," the boy giggled.

"Oh yes, I have a funny, name but can you spell it, Gabriel. Do you want to give it a try? You do know your alphabet, don't you?"

"My father taught me well. I didn't know it, but all those years he was preparing me for this day. I know my alphabet."

"Yes, Gabriel! Can you at least give it a try? Come on."

"Okay, I'll give it a try Fineous. F-i-n-n-e-u-s! There. How'd I do, Mr. Fineous?"

"Wonderful Gabriel, you tried. Dear Gabriel, you are intuitive and bright. The way I pronounced my name, you heard and regurgitated as you thought to be correct. The lesson was not whether you could get it right, but could you try in front of a man of the metropolis and stand on your own two feet. You did, and for that, I will reveal to you a great secret about myself. But first, I must know, do you respect me?"

"My father taught me to respect everyman as if they were equal," said Gabriel feeling more at ease.

"So, are we equal, Gabriel? Do you see us as equals?"

Yes," he said. Gabriel explained to Mr. Riley that before this, his father was his teacher, and he told him that no man was better than him. Some men are better at some things than others. In the same right, others are better than those men at things; we're all different. So, if you wanted to ask him, were they equal? Knowing he is better at things than you, and you are better at things than he is in some right, then yes, we are equals, he thought, at least in this partnership.

"Gabriel, you are a truly amazing six-year-old. Now, let me reveal something about myself to you," said Mr. Riley. "I told you I was an alumnus of this school, but what I did not tell you is that I am retired from my job in the heart of the city. I teach here ten hours a week and only to special students. This socialization course is to bring you up to speed, let you know how the people of the Metropolis think. Do you think you are up to that task Gabriel?"

"I want to be, and besides, I don't have a choice, do I," asked Gabriel listening intently?

"There is always a choice Gabriel. You can choose to do poorly or you can excel in your learning. Gabriel, when I came to this school, I had a similar choice: sink or swim. Would you like to know why you and I are not so different? Would you, Gabriel?"

"Yes, Mr. Fineous. I'd like to know," said Gabriel perking up as he listened.

"I too was on an academic scholarship from the uptown part of the metropolis, said Mr. Riley. "In other words, Gabriel, the board allows me to teach this class to two students a year, sometimes only one, however. I will never reveal to the other students about you. Your secrecy is paramount to your success, it was paramount to my success as well. And Gabriel, I remember my early youth in the outer parts as you will someday, but I did learn my life was better because of this school. Perhaps you'd like to reveal something about yourself now, Gabriel."

"I don't know what you want me to say, Mr. Fineous. I was always told I was simple but smart."

"Tell me about your parents," asked Mr. Riley, intertwining his fingers into a double fist?

"I'd rather not," said Gabriel in a defensive tone.

"Then something else perhaps," said Mr. Riley.

"I like what sports I have played, though I do not know them all. I am very good at catch, Mr. Fineous."

"We have the best baseball team in the metropolis! We even have youth programs for your age Gabriel. Does that excite you? It should."

"I have a question, Mr. Fineous," asked Gabriel, unknowingly leaning forward in his chair?

"Yes, son."

"Why did your parents place you here? Why did you come to this school? There is a simple answer that is not so simple," said Mr. Riley. "When I was a young man about the age of nine or ten, my father inherited money from his great uncle who lived in the metropolis. My father saw that gift as a sign to make his life better. My father sold his orchards and moved the family to the uptown district of the metropolis. My father's great uncle's son, my father's cousin, had attended this very school some years earlier. As someone who was born in the city, not the country, he was able to pull some strings and get me in. At the time Richard Massey was the socialization teacher, himself once a country child. So, the short of the long is that my father loved me that is why he put me here. He wanted a better life for me."

"Yes, but that's not why my father put me here. He put me here because he does not want me," said Gabriel with a distressed look on his face.

Mr. Riley stroked his long beard and addressed the young boy saying, "On the contrary, Gabriel, your father put you here because he loves you. I've spoken with your father Gabriel, his wish for you is to make a grand man out of yourself. He wants you to love him, maybe even let him visit you now and then to see what life would be like if his father had done the same for him," said Mr. Riley interlocking his hands and placing them on top of his calendar.

"Well, I don't ever want to see him again; he abandoned me. He does not love me. He wants me to fancy him a better life, well I'll show him. I'll become a great man, but I will not love him and include him in my life. I'll show him Mr. Fineous."

Mr. Riley explained to Gabriel that those in the city have better lives than those in the outer parts. That is why his father sent him there. Spite has made many a man great, but pride would serve him better, he said. Whether he wished to include his father in his life is his prerogative, but as someone who has seen both the metropolis and outer parts, he asked him to listen to him about this new life and his new opportunity. So if it pleased, they would move forward, father or not.

"Very well then, Mr. Fineous, I'll listen," said Gabriel perking up.

"Good, Gabriel, I'm excited. Now the first thing we've got to do is rid you of that accent the outer parts gave you, teach how to pronounce like a man from the metropolis, not the country. Okay, Gabriel, repeat after me..."

Mr. Riley and Gabriel sat for the remainder of their first hour practicing the correct pronunciation of the alphabet, trying to get rid of that outer part drawl he had. Over and over, they worked repeating the words in which he had trouble. Gabriel was a quick and eager learner, but eventually, the session came to a close, and Gabriel left and headed for his next class where he would meet Arthur.

He met Arthur, and they discussed Mr. Riley and his past life. Arthur wasn't surprised. The physical education class went off without a hitch. Gabriel was a fit young boy. The two of them ran around the track, doing some light exercise like jumping jacks and pushups, knee bends, and toe touches. All of these exercises Gabriel was more than capable of doing. In fact, he excelled at them. The rest of the day continued much like the next few weeks would with English, mathematics, and science, once again.

Gabriel continued with Mr. Riley through the weeks to follow and found he increasingly excelled in English and writing. His scores in his other subjects were notable as well. Arthur and Gabriel's friendship grew as the year progressed. The two were thick as thieves, best friends as it was. They enjoyed their class together, as well as lunch, and the hours after class.

Through this period in Gabriel's life, he had all but buried his feelings for his father; his mother, on the other hand, was another story. He had not talked to her in many months. He longed to have a glass of tea with her on the front porch or play hide and seek in the fields. It's true. He had not forgotten his mother. He didn't know how she would receive him if they met. He hoped for loving arms.

September, October, and November passed, December finally coming around, and the boy started to wonder what he would do for the break. His classes with Mr. Riley were a huge success. His therapy had paid off. Repetition after repetition of those old words had made him feel lesser of a child. It had now made him feel confident. The semester was ending, and Gabriel's marks in his classes were well above average. The children of these parts were indeed advanced, and Gabriel fit right in. The time of finals approached; Gabriel and Arthur both studied hard. Gabriel had acclimated to the new life he had been given. He was very thankful for what he had. However, he still could not find it in his heart to forgive his father, though he always longed to see his mother.

Suddenly, one morning around eight-thirty, just before class, someone knocked on his door. He answered. There stood Mr. Riley, beard and all, explaining that his parents were on the phone. He jumped to attention and headed out the door. They took a short ride on the golf cart down the cobblestone street. They made it to Mr. Riley's office, and there in front of him, as with every day, was the same phone he had distracted him often. Mr. Riley picked up the phone and said, "Can you patch the Liden's through, Alice. Now, Gabriel, you choose what you want to say carefully. You're a man of the metropolis now. Talk to them as if they love you."

"Alright, give me the phone," said Gabriel. He reluctantly put the phone to his ear and cleared his throat, "Hello, this is Gabriel."

"Gabriel, it's your mama, Anne! Can you hear me, honey?"

"Yes, mother, I can hear you," said Gabriel switching ears.

"Gabriel I'm so sorry we haven't talked to you in so long they wouldn't let us," said Anne.

Suddenly, a cold voice came on the line, "Please keep your conversation positive, The Highland Boys School has never kept anyone from contacting their sons. Please continue your conversation."

"Gabriel, are you alright?" asked Anne.

"Yes, mother, I'm fine."

"Why do you call me mother, honey," said Anne. "I'm your mama, baby, don't you remember? Don't you remember? Baby, how are you? Gabriel, your father wants to speak with you. Will you talk with him?"

"I don't wish to speak to my father at this juncture; I'm sorry, mother," said Gabriel holding back tears of pain and sorrow, trying to be the man they all wanted him to be.

"Gabriel, we'd like to have you come home to the country for Christmas," said Anne.

"The Highland Boys School has already made arrangements for the holidays for Mr. Gabriel Liden," said the cold voice on the line.

"After all mother it's not a good idea, we're different now. Perhaps some other time we can get together," said Gabriel holding back his emotions. He wanted to cry. He wanted to yell, but mostly he wanted to hug his mother and sister desperately.

"Won't you please reconsider talking with your father; this is not how he pictured things going. We love you, dearly, Gabriel."

"I think its best we keep at a distance for now mother, and as for father, perhaps we'll talk in the future, but I have nothing to say to him now."

"Don't you think you should at least say thank you to him? He has sacrificed a lot for you, Gabriel," said Anne.

"Yes. Give father my thanks for abandoning me. I have to go now," said Gabriel. "Goodbye, for now, mother."

"Okay, Gabriel, if that's the way you want it. We'll talk later, in a few months. I'll give your father your love," said Anne.

"If you must, now goodbye, mother," said Gabriel.

"Bye," said Anne, lamenting as her husband sank into his regretful world in the background, wishing he could see his son.

The cold voice came on the line, "Thank you for calling the Highland Boys School, have a nice day."

Mr. Riley hung up the phone for Gabriel and sat in his chair and began to smoke his pipe. "Gabriel," he said, "I'm proud of you. You stood the ground for what you thought was right. You spoke like a man. Your diction was beautiful, and most of all, you held back that part of you that just wanted to break down and cry. I could see it in your eyes."

"What was that voice on the line?"

"All outer parts calls are monitored to make sure there is well, no propaganda. Do you know what propaganda is Gabriel," asked Mr. Riley?

"You mean they're trying to get me to believe something like I want to go back to the outer parts. You told me one day, Mr. Fineous, that it is better not to visit as a child, I should wait until I'm older. Isn't that right, Mr. Fineous?"

"Yes, Gabriel, when you can handle your emotions better, even though you handled them wonderfully today," said Mr. Riley stroking his beard as he inhaled his tobacco.

"Mr. Fineous, the voice on the line said that there were already arrangements for me for the holidays. I didn't know anything about this. Where am I going," asked Gabriel?

"A board member has arranged for you to go to his house for the holidays."

"What board member?" he asked.

"Why Mr. Highland, of course. You'll be spending the time with Arthur and his family for many holidays to come," said Mr. Riley.

"Arthur didn't tell me. Are you sure, Mr. Fineous?"

"Oh, I'm quite positive. I did something similar with the Highland family generations ago," said Mr. Riley. He explained they take in one new child from the outer parts when they have a boy in school. For years they had a succession of girls born into the family. The Highland family was not pleased. Arthur is the first boy in many years. Just like they took him in when Arthur's great grandfather was on the board, and his son attended, so shall they do with him. "Are you excited, Gabriel? You get to live in the midtown district for a month. It's been years since I was there, but I believe it will still be as beautiful as it ever was."

"Mr. Fineous it's true, Artie is my best friend, but why would they take me in?"

"Well, for Artie's sake, as you call him, to be a Highland means to be a well-rounded and a complete gentleman. You are a humble child, Gabriel; you come from very humble beginnings. The Highlands have always been kind to people with such attributes as yours. The Highlands have money, but they are also philanthropic people. Do you understand what that means, Gabriel?"

"They want to help people," said Gabriel with a true sense of innocence.

"Yes, son," said Mr. Riley. "They want to help you. Please take whatever help this family offers you, especially since all the board and staff know you and Arthur are great friends."

"They don't pity me do they, Mr. Riley," asked Gabriel in an insecure tone of voice?

"There are some at this school who would pity you, Gabriel," said Mr. Riley, "The headmaster may be one of those people, but the Highlands have your best interest at heart. Arthur has your best interest at heart. Now, if you don't hurry, you'll be late for your finals, Gabriel, so you'd better go."

"But what about my final with you, Mr. Riley, my second final isn't until ten. It's only nine-thirty," said Gabriel looking wide-eyed and eager.

"This is not a pass or fail class, Gabriel. But if you'd like a final, perhaps you can answer this. What do you want to be when you grow up," asked Mr. Riley.

"If you would have asked me that question four months ago," said Gabriel, "I would have said a farmer or just maybe... I don't know. But learning the things I have learned with you during this time, perhaps I'd like to be a writer; I enjoy language and words. I'd like to be an uptowner or maybe even live in midtown someday. Of course. I'd like to be a gentleman and a scholar, Mr. Fineous."

"Gabriel, nothing makes me happier than for you to say those words," said Mr. Riley. "If there were a grade for this class, you would have a one hundred and bright shining stars. We have another semester together next year, but you have already learned most of what you need to know. There is no hint of an accent in your voice and, you already are a gentleman Gabriel. Oh! and yes, you're well on your way to being a scholar if those grades come in as expected."

"Thank you, Mr. Fineous. I'm glad I didn't let you down," said Gabriel with a satisfied child-like smile.

"Gabriel, you have fifteen minutes to get to your physical education final. I'm sure you'll make excellent marks," said Mr. Riley. "Go tell Arthur you know you're coming home with him for the holidays. He'll be glad we've let you know. Now go before you're late, Gabriel. Go with a strong sense of accomplishment, and know you have grown immensely. Go now, Gabriel, enjoy the next day or so and study hard."

"Very well, sir, and thank you once again," said Gabriel. "I'll see you next semester."

"Bye now, Gabriel," said Mr. Riley.

Gabriel ran to his next final, where he met Arthur and broke the news that he knew of his and his father's intentions, Arthur was relieved. The two boys had their final. They did the most pushups, the most pull-ups, and ran the fastest times in the mile, no doubt a team. The two boys showered, Gabriel now more comfortable with communal showers, and the two went for lunch.

"I'm glad you're coming home with us, Gabe," said Arthur.

"Me too," said Gabriel. "I honestly never gave a thought to where I was going. I thought maybe I might be staying with Mr. Fineous, but this turn of events is amazing! Midtown, I can't wait. Mr. Fineous has told me all about midtown, but where exactly do you live."

"My parents own the top floor of the Metropolitan Plaza," said Arthur.

"The Metropolitan Plaza," asked Gabriel? "That's the nicest hotel in the metropolis! You mean, I get to stay there?"

"Yup," said Arthur! "We even have servants, Gabe. There's Angela, she helps cook. Bethany does most of the cleaning, and of course, there's Mr. Johnstone, the butler. He lets me call him James; he's my favorite."

"Do you think they'll like me," said Gabriel. "I mean, will they know I'm from the outer parts?"

"Of course, they will. But don't ever tell anyone this Gabe, all our help is from the outer parts," said Arthur. "They all moved to the city after their formal education, and my parents just took them in, well as formal as their education gets. I don't mean that in a bad way, Gabe, they just don't learn the same things we do. For instance, Angela didn't learn to cook in school, she just learned from her mother, and boy can she cook. Then James is just the greatest guy. He knows a lot about vegetables, fruits, and meats. He especially knows about all the locations in the city, so he does most of the shopping for us. And Bethany, well, she's just a great homemaker, very meticulous, keeps things spotless."

Gabriel was teeming with excitement. He'd forgotten all about the phone call he had just had. Midtown was like a fairy tale to him, only he knew it well; Mr. Riley had described it well. Arthur began telling Gabriel more about the metropolis and midtown. Gabriel couldn't get enough. Only four months ago Gabriel knew nothing about the metropolis, only that his kind didn't go there. Now he was about to be staying in the wealthiest and most posh area of town. The boys went back to their room and began studying for their finals the next day. Gabriel had the remaining four finals left; English, Science, Math, and History. Arthur's were also similar for his last day. They studied hard and made an early night of it. Arthur was busy giving more stories of the metropolis to Gabriel, especially his favorite area: the uptown area.

The sleep that night was deep and long, but the early morning came eventually. They both woke, showered, and made it to their finals. They both thought they did well, but only time would tell. As the day ended, the boys went back to their room and packed for the month ahead. Arthur kept joking with Gabriel telling him he was going to fall in love with Angela. She was quite good-looking, and oh, her pies and cakes. Her pies and cakes were amazing. There was cherry pie, apple pie, cheesecake, and of course, his favorite: red velvet cake. Gabriel had never had red velvet cake, so he was almost too excited to taste it, he thought. Nonetheless, the boys finished packing and made their way out to the cobblestone streets. A limousine was waiting for them, they got in the car, and the vacation began. Explore and have fun Gabriel...

Chapter 3

Home

The car ride was long. It was rush hour in the metropolis, but the boys made the most of it. Gabriel asked Arthur a long list of questions of Arthur He wanted to know where they would go first, what time they had to be home each day, and would they travel throughout the city or just in midtown?

Arthur laughed, "Gabe, we have the city at our disposal. You just wait. There is plenty to see and we have a whole month," said Arthur.

The boys arrived in the midtown district around sunset; Gabriel was teeming with excitement. Just one year ago, he had not even known of the city, much less the midtown area. He was in awe as they pulled up to the Metropolitan Plaza. It was a beautiful old building, some forty stories tall. A row of gargoyles lined the sides of the building. The New Atlanta Metropolis flag was flying in front of the building, along with four others Gabriel did not recognize. The windows were tall and wide, arching, and marking every floor.

The boy's car pulled into the hotel's roundabout, and two bellhops ran eagerly to the vehicle. One went to the rear door of the passenger side, and the other to the trunk of their limousine, fetching their luggage. The door opened, and a young man poked his head in and said,

"Hello, and welcome to the Metropolitan Plaza."

"Hello, Bartleby," said Arthur.

"Oh, Mr. Highland! Good to see you. We didn't expect you until tomorrow. What a nice surprise, though," said Bartleby, the bellhop.

"Well, Bartleby, this year we left right after finals. We didn't leave with all the others. By the way, has my father arrived," asked Arthur?

"No, not yet, but I see you have company, Arthur," said the bellhop.

"Sorry for being so rude Bartleby, this is Gabriel Liden. He is in his first year at the school. He'll be staying with us this holiday," said Arthur.

"I don't mean to pry Mr. Highland, but is he, well, you know, one of us?"

"He's on scholarship if that's what you're asking, Bartleby."

"Well then, hello, Mr. Liden, what a pleasure. As you can probably tell by now, my name is Bartleby, Bartleby Stone, and I am at your service."

"Hello Mr. Bartleby," said Gabriel extending his hand. "I'm pleased to make your acquaintance, but please call me Gabriel, Mr. Liden seems so formal. I'm only six, you know."

"Well then, six-year-old Gabriel Liden, welcome to the Metropolitan Plaza, we're all glad to have you," said the bellhop Bartleby.

Gabriel thanked the young man, and the boys stepped out onto the somewhat familiar cobblestone roundabout. They made their way to the entrance of the building. In front of them was a beautiful antique revolving door that greeted all the guests. Gabriel walked forward towards the door and couldn't resist. He raced into the door and went around a few times. After all, this was his first revolving door. He had only seen them in books. Arthur just laughed as he watched his friend's face brighten through each of the turns he made.

On the third go-around, Gabriel finally made it to the inside of the plaza; Arthur was waiting patiently. The lobby, adorned with beautiful giant marble columns, reminded Gabriel of the ancient columns he knew from school. Gabriel had seen them in the books Mr. Riley had shown him in class, but as often happens, the pictures did them no justice. To the left was the concierge. There were three young persons that gave a tip of the hat to Arthur and Gabriel as they made it to the elevators. Walking on the marble white, gold-encrusted floor, Gabriel had a feeling that everything was going to be okay this holiday. As they stepped into the elevator, an older gentleman sat holding the controls to the large moving room.

"This is my first elevator ride with operated controls, Artie," said Gabriel looking at all the buttons and controls.

"Don't worry, Gabe," said Arthur. "Clarence here is the best elevator operator in the whole of the metropolis. He's smooth and quick. By the way, Clarence, this is Gabriel Liden, but I like to call him Gabe, so I guess you can too."

Clarence didn't say a word. He just looked over with his old blue eyes, and his grey mustache and tipped his red and brown circular hat. He raised the brass gate and set the controls for the top floor. Clarence didn't say a word the whole ride, all forty stories. Gabriel was puzzled as his ears began popping; he thought how curious this was. Clarence didn't even move or touch his ears; what a strange man this Clarence fellow was.

They reached the fortieth floor, and Clarence's withered hands opened the gate and then the door to the elevator. The two boys stepped out into a small hallway, which was only about twelve feet long and eight feet wide, beautifully decorated, and meticulously cleaned; the two proceeded to the doorway just in front of them. Arthur rustled through his bag, looking for his key, but before he could find it, the door opened.

"Oh, Arthur! It's so good to see you," said Angela. "And you must be Gabriel, we've heard so much about you from Mr. Highland. He says you're very bright. Well, let me take a look at you. Oh, you're going to be a looker like Arthur here. Mr. Highland is going to be late, so I've prepared some dinner for the two of you. Goodness! What am I saying, boys? Where are my manners? Come on in, you two. Boys let me take your coats, normally James would be doing this Gabriel, but he's out running errands now, so I'll just have to do."

"You'll do just fine, miss Angela," said Gabriel.

"Oh, how cute! You must have picked the "miss" thing up from the outer parts. They haven't excised that out of you yet," said Angela motioning them inside.

"Angela, we all know where Gabe is from, but let's keep that talk to a minimum, shall we," said Arthur removing his black coat. "It's for the best, Angela."

"Yes, Arthur, I'm sorry. Anyway, let's go eat now."

The boys stepped into a mid-century modern haven. Mr. Highland had an affinity for the modern and the contemporary of the past. The house was done in muted colors and scattered with what Gabriel deemed to be odd-shaped furniture; he liked it nonetheless. They went through the large open space and into a clean, white, and wooden kitchen. The two boys sat at a small nook in the corner of the room and served Arthur's favorite meal: country ham and grits. It was a delicacy for the young boy. Angela learned how to cook it when she was quite young in the outer parts. Gabriel felt at home eating a meal his mother might have even cooked for him. But suddenly, memories sparked, and he remembered his phone call. He was not able to just talk with his mother how he used to; it was different now, distant.

"What's wrong, Gabriel," asked Angela looking up from the stove? "You look sad."

"It's nothing, I just miss my mother all of a sudden," said Gabriel. "This meal reminds me of something she would cook. Don't get me wrong it's wonderful Angela, thank you. I mean that from the bottom of my heart."

"I'm sorry I've made you sad, dear Gabriel. It's just that this is Arthur's favorite meal. I didn't think it would bother you," said Angela. "I'd be glad to cook you something else, Gabriel. If it makes you feel any better, when I used to miss my mother, I could remember this beautiful song she would sing to me. When she was happy, she would sing it to me, and soon I would be singing it to myself happy as a lark. When I sing it, the words are always changing around. I didn't know most of the words she sang. I was so little, but it did the job anyway when I got blue. It never failed. I was always singing jubilantly in two or three minutes. Did your mom ever sing you anything, Gabriel?"

"She liked to sing mockingbird a lot," said Gabriel. "She had the most pleasant voice. I usually fell asleep within a few minutes, but I was happy."

"Would you like me to sing it to you, Gabriel," asked Angela with a smile on her face?

"No, let's just have some fun, that's why we're all here, isn't it," said Gabriel.

"Exactly Gabe, we don't have to have grits and ham anymore if you don't want to. Angela, do you have any pies or cakes in the house?" asked Arthur.

"Does a goose fly south in the winter, dear boy?" said Angela. "I have several scrumptious ones from which to choose. Now Gabriel, in case you didn't know it, Arthur here's favorite cake is red velvet, of which I have one, but perhaps your favorite will be a cobbler or a cheesecake. I have a candied cheesecake made with real cookies, or I have a cherry cobbler. Which will it be?"

"Well," said Gabriel, "I've had cobbler before but never a cookie cheesecake. However, I must say I'm looking forward to the red velvet. So, can I have both?"

"Of course, you can, Gabe," said Arthur. "In fact, Angela, let's have one of each just to try. Gabe here needs a warm welcome, an idea of what he'll find while he's here."

"Very well then Arthur, you and Gabriel shall have one of each of them," said Angela. "We shall eat like hogs, but we must hurry, Mr. Highland will be home soon. He probably wouldn't approve."

The boys enjoyed the pies and cakes, but rather quickly I'm afraid; Mr. Highland would be home shortly. Gabriel had never formally met Mr. Highland. He had seen him once or twice walking around the school, always giving tours, probably not unlike the one Mr. Liden took. But it was dark then, and the boys were enjoying their sugar rushes. Angela entertained the boys until the front door opened; it was James. Arthur rushed to the door and gave him a big hug. James affectionately embraced the boy, patting him on the head. "What did you get me, James? James always brings presents, Gabriel," said Arthur.

"First, Arthur, your manners," said James taking off his coat and hat. "I believe introductions are in order."

"Oh, yes! James, this is Gabriel Liden, but I like to call him Gabe, James," said Arthur.

"Liden? Of the western Liden Farms group," inquired James looking toward young Gabriel?

"That's my father and mother," said Gabriel with a sudden sense of waning pride.

"Your father grows good produce and other such things. I know where the farms are, I grew up not far from there."

"It was nice while I was there, but I'm better off without them," said Gabriel looking back down.

"Do you actually believe that Gabriel, that you are better off without your parents," asked James? "They may not have the same opportunities you've been presented with, but that doesn't make them bad people. Mr. Highland himself will tell you that you should embrace the metropolis, but never forget where you come from."

"Mr. Fineous says I shouldn't look back," said Gabriel briefly looking up then back down.

"I've met Mr. Fineous Riley, and if he were here outside of that class of his, he would tell you not to forget your roots. They make you well-rounded."

"My roots involve my father, and he does not love me anymore, so I do not love him," said Gabriel.

"I will say this, young Gabriel. Perhaps your perception is skewed because of your age and recent events. You're still adjusting. Somewhere in your future, you will find you'll have to come to terms with whether you love your father for giving you what he has given you, or hate him because you feel he abandoned you. You'll decide. Good. Well, that is all I wish to say about that. Now! Presents."

James pulled out two identical wool hats, merino wool to be exact, and the boys grabbed them and placed them on their heads. They were a perfectly snug fit all around the boy's heads, black and chic, just the things to keep the boys warm during their adventures through the city this coming month. Arthur and Gabriel thanked James. Gabriel almost too much thought Arthur. James told them to ready themselves for the evening discussion with Arthur's father.

The boys ran to their room, unpacked their clothing, and dressed for the occasion. Black hats, of course, on their heads, Gabriel inquired as to what the evening discussion would be? Arthur explained that every semester he and his father sat down and discussed what they had learned. Gabriel would be in this year's discussion and all future times from now on.

The ten o'clock hour was upon them. Arthur heard a familiar voice out in the foyer. He rushed to meet his parents, both of them in from taking care of some hotel business. "Hello father, hello mother," Arthur said jubilantly. James took the Highland's coats and retired to the back of the house. Gabriel stood there sheepishly as his best friend was enveloped with such a warm welcome.

"Arthur, we are being rude. Gabriel, come here boy," said Mr. Highland motioning to him.

Gabriel walked shyly over to the huddled family. He remembered his own family and how they had once embraced him as such. "It is customary to give all guests a warm welcome into our home Gabriel, so don't be shy," said Mr. Highland.

Gabriel reached out for the unfamiliar fatherly hug, wishing it could be his father. It felt good, the love of an adult, someone who had his best interests at heart. They hugged for a moment, and Gabriel then felt the need to let go. The boy had very good feelings at that moment. He knew he was safe.

"Gabriel," said Mr. Highland. "Have our friends here at our home made you feel welcome?"

"Of course, they have father," said Arthur.

"Arthur, I believe I asked Gabriel that question," said Mr. Highland. "So, Gabriel, have you been welcomed properly?"

"Oh yes sir, Angela, and James have been more than wonderful, but I have yet to meet Bethany, sir. I'm told she keeps the place tidy."

"Please don't call me Sir, Gabriel, it makes me feel old. My full name is Ignatious Hawthorne Highland, and the Boys in the hotel call me Haw, so if you feel comfortable enough, call me Haw. If not, if you insist, then call me Mr. Highland."

"Yes, Haw," giggled Gabriel.

"Oh! You think that's funny, do you, Gabriel? It kind of sounds like paw doesn't it. You can think of me as your paw, as those from the outer parts might say. If you'd like to, I know it seems rather soon, but you're a part of this family now. Well, you just keep that in mind now, us welcoming you into our family, I mean. But nonetheless, that's my nickname, Gabriel. The great Ignatious Haw the Paw, that's what they called me when I played for the Highland baseball team; I was the best outfielder the school had ever seen. Now, I believe it's time for a little family tradition. It's time for our end-of-the-semester discussion. Gabriel, since you are the newest to the family, why don't you follow us to the living room."

Gabriel did as he was asked and moved to the living room. He sat on one of those oddly shaped couches and tried to make himself as comfortable as possible. He didn't really know what to expect. "So, boys! Would you say it was a good year or a bad year," said Mr. Highland. Gabriel was hesitant to answer, but Arthur blurted out, "It was wonderful, father!"

"What made it so wonderful, Arthur," asked Mr. Highland?

"I have a new best friend and brother," said Arthur curling up on the couch and getting comfortable.

"Would you agree, Gabriel, that it too has been wonderful," asked Mr. Highland?

"I've indeed gained a friend, unlike any I've ever known, but I have also lost, Haw," said Gabriel.

"You speak of your old family, I presume," said Mr. Highland. "Gabriel, your father wanted a better life for you. He didn't tell you that from the start, in doing that, he was wrong. Before you were even born, your father was plotting a life away from him. He wanted for you a new life in the metropolis. He may have meant well, but as you've learned in socialization class, it is better to be cut off from that old part of your life and embrace the new; you must see that."

"He planned it from the beginning, you say," said Gabriel. "You say that, but how do I know it wasn't something I did."

"Your father came to my school and me six years ago looking for an avenue for a better life for you, and we obliged him.

We agreed to take his son in, but even as much as we love the outer parts, we are still from the metropolis. Unlike some, we are kind and know those that want to make a better life can if they try. You remember Bartleby, he spent twenty years in the outer parts and moved himself to the downtown district and eventually heard that we were sympathetic and now he lives a good life, better than the one he was living in the country. Do you see why you are here, Gabriel?"

"Yes and no. Was my father trying to make a better life for me or himself?"

"Only God knows, Gabriel. I can understand if you think you hate your father, but in our lives, we say forgiveness is the greatest way. But you can choose your own fate, live and dream with us, freely, or forge a road of hatred towards your father. But whatever you decide, tonight is not the night to make that decision. You have a month in our home, and you will have many more months in our home. I implore you to make the best of your youth. God knows that without a good childhood, you will spend your adult life searching endlessly for something you may never find. So, what do you say Gabriel, will you enjoy your time here?"

"Yes Haw, thank you for taking me in, sincerely," said Gabriel.

"Good then, son, let's move on."

Arthur began telling of his stories with Gabriel and how his classes went to his father. Gabriel seemed very thoughtful but seemed to enjoy himself throughout the conversation. The three talked well into the eleven o'clock hour. Arthur ever so often nudged Gabriel giving an all-knowing smile. Eventually, the three had exhausted themselves with a long day of finals, pies, and cakes, and of course, the discussion at the end of the night. Mr. Highland instructed Arthur to take him to Lordes Department store and get him some proper dress. He told him to spare no expense, just use the house account. The boys said their goodnights and made their way to the bedroom—this time for a well-deserved night of slumber.

It was a cold winter night, but the boys were safe and warm in the penthouse of the hotel, Gabriel dreaming of the day ahead, Arthur thankful for his best friend. Gabriel dreamed of his father that night. He dreamed the two went to play catch by the fields again, but there was no ball to be found. Suddenly, as most nights end, the buzz of the alarm clock rang nine o'clock. The boys wished for more slumber, but then they both realized they were not at school anymore. Instead, they were in the heart of midtown, and they both sprang to their feet. They walked into the hallway and Gabriel was caught by an unfamiliar face.

"Hello," he said.

"Oh Gabriel, this is the famed Bethany. Say hello, Bethany," said Arthur motioning toward Gabriel.

"I can only assume that you are Gabriel. It is a pleasure to meet you, the Highland family speaks very highly of you," said Bethany.

"You're very pretty Bethany, Arthur didn't warn me," said Gabriel. "He said he was in love with Angel..."

"Whoa, whoa, whoa! No one's in love with Angela. He doesn't know what he's talking about Bethany," said Arthur.

"And to think, all this time, Arthur, I thought you had a thing for me. Okay, now I see, well Angela is waiting in the kitchen for you two, you'd better go," said Bethany.

"I hope to see you again, Bethany," said Gabriel, "I'm a pretty good cleaner, you know, maybe I could help you straighten up one morning."

"You just hold on to that little crush for a girl from the Guild Hall or maybe even The Midtown Girls School, it would probably serve you better. But if you really want to help me straighten up, I won't discourage you," said Bethany dusting a small figurine on the hall desk.

"Bethany, you're my second favorite, you know," said Arthur. "But Gabriel won't have any time to be cleaning; we have a city to explore. Come on, Gabe!"

The boys made their way to the kitchen to what would become that old familiar nook and ate pancakes, eggs, and bacon to the fill. Then the boys made their way to the bathroom and showered. Arthur let Gabriel borrow some of last year's clothes so he wouldn't look out of place in the posh midtown district. They suited up, black hats and all, and headed for the car waiting downstairs. They met Clarence in the elevator, once again saying nothing and then down through the revolving door. "Straight to Lordes," Arthur said to the driver, and the two were off.

Gabriel's face was pressed against the window, looking at all the sights he had seen in his socialization books. They passed the restaurant Sol Y Luna, the metropolitan springs, and the Museum of Cultural Arts. The ride was only a matter of minutes, and the time was now ten-thirty. The driver got out and opened the door for the boys. They headed into the department store. The building was several stories high, and a large wishing fountain welcomed all who entered. The entrance was the start of the endless makeup counters and young men and women offering wishes of youth and vitality to all of the wealthy that entered its lobby. Just beyond the entrance of the threshold of the store, he saw all the departments on the map. Gabriel looked for a moment and said, "Let's go to the sports department."

"No time," said Arthur, "We're set for a fitting or two.

The boys made it up to the young men's department on the second floor, and they were greeted by two salesmen. "Do you gentlemen need any help," asked one of the men?

Arthur proudly boasted his chest and said, "I'm Arthur Highland, and this is my friend Gabriel. We need some clothes to last a month; no expense spared," said the young boy.

"Well then, Mr. Highland, we shall find you the finest of clothing and footwear," said the other salesmen with a brief snide look to his colleague.

The boys started in the suit department. They would need some for their nights with their father and mother. Lordes had all the designers, all of which Gabriel had learned of in school. The suits were thousands of dollars, and then they were on to the fine leather shoes, then coats and shirts. The boys then made it to the casual wear, the finest of jeans, the game shirts, and the most hi-tech running shoes. The boys shopped for hours, Gabriel amazed at the whimsical spending of Arthur, but he thought, this too shall be my way of life.

"Put it on the Highland tab," the boys said again and again and again until they had so much clothing and so many boxes of shoes, they could not carry them all. Arthur told one of the salesmen he would add a hundred dollars for him if he would have the clothes delivered to The Metropolitan Plaza. The clothes are going to the penthouse, he said. The concierge will know where they go.

"Gabriel," Arthur said looking over the mound of clothing. "There is somewhere I want to show you. Come now."

The boys left the department store and headed for the car. The driver pulled around and asked, "Where to Mr. Highland?"

"Uptown," said Arthur. Gabriel looked puzzled. He was under the impression he was going to be seeing the midtown district that day. Nonetheless, the driver pulled off. They went down Holmstead Avenue, then turned on to Commons Place. They stayed on Commons until they reached Virginia Avenue, the heart of Uptown. Arthur told the driver to park, and the two boys got out.

"Why did you take me here, Artie," asked Gabriel closing his coat as they left the car?

"Midtown is for rich old people, but uptown, Virginia Avenue is where the common people hang out. There are arcades, candy shops, and of course, hotdog vendors. Have you ever had a metropolis hot dog, Gabe? I can answer that, no, you haven't. This is where the real action is. We're anonymous here. We're just two kids out to have a good time. It's one-thirty now why don't we get a hot dog?"

"Okay, Artie, if you say so," said Gabriel finishing zipping his coat and adjusting his scarf and hat.

The anonymous young men walked down Virginia Avenue until Artie spotted his favorite hot dog stand. They bellied up to the two seats at the stand and said, "Two dogs and give 'em the works, please." The boys devoured their food, belching, and sipping their cola's living as an uptown child would. Arthur so longed for the mediocrity and anonymity of the uptown while Gabriel was just becoming accustomed to the life of a rich man. The truth of the matter was that Gabriel was just beginning his journey. He didn't know where it would take him or where it would end. The boys finished their hot dogs and headed to the candy shop, where they picked and ate candy for half an hour. Gabriel made the comment that he was sure he had a cavity as the two sugar rushed children made it to the arcade.

Gabriel had never played a video game. He was awkward at first, but he was a quick learner and soon was scoring high scores; Arthur just cheered him on. The boy had lost his father and mother and sister but had gained surrogate parents who could offer him a better life, not to mention the undying companionship of Arthur. Gabriel posed the question to himself that day, a little paradox. If he had never gone to the metropolis, had he never left the outer parts, would he have had the thought that he needed a better life? But the other part of that puzzle lies in knowing that he would never know if it was better or worse. He only knew he was where he was then, and that was a long way from the corn and tobacco fields of the outer parts.

It was getting late in the day, and the boys were starting to feel a little tired, so they started back towards the car. They passed a few jewelry stores and an outdoor-outfitters with a sign that read, tours of the outer part mountains every weekend. But then the boys walked past a curious little shop and Gabriel was intrigued. "What are these," asked Gabriel.

"Well, those are bikes, of course, Gabe. Haven't you ever seen one," said Arthur laughing just a little bit.

"They look different in person, I mean... What are they for," asked Gabriel looking over the bicycles?

"Well, they're for getting around, but they're also for having fun. Hold on, wait a minute," said Arthur.

Arthur went into the shopkeeper and explained that his friend had never ridden a bike, could he help him show him how. The shopkeeper was proud to help two young boys, such as Gabriel and Arthur. So he pulled out a young man's bike, readied it with some training wheels, and brought it out to the curb. Gabriel asked, "Well, what do I do?"

Arthur replied, "Just put your feet on the pedals and push. Go ahead, Gabe."

Gabriel pushed his feet to the pedal on the right, and it went forward naturally, bringing up the left; he pushed it down. Soon he was on his way down the street teetering between the two training wheels, but he felt amazing. "You're right, Arthur. It's faster than walking, and it is fun too," said Gabriel with a grand smile on his face. What no one told Gabriel was how to stop the thing. So, he barreled into a shopkeeper's fruit bin just down the way, wrecking the bike and falling somewhat hard to the ground. Arthur and the bicycle shopkeeper went running down the sidewalk to where Gabriel and the other shopkeeper were.

"Gabe, are you alright," exclaimed Arthur!

"Yes, son. Are you okay? You took a nasty little spill," said the shopkeeper.

"I didn't know how to stop it, oh my head. But I loved it."

"That's great, kid," said the bicycle shopkeeper, "But someone's got to pay for this damage to both this gentleman's cart and my bike."

"I'll take care of this," said Arthur.

"No, wait, Artie. How much for the bike, Mr. shopkeeper," asked Gabriel?

"One hundred and fifty. Do you think you boys have that kind of money," asked the shopkeeper?

"We don't have that kind of money, sir, but we're really sorry," explained Arthur helping Gabriel to his feet and helping dust him off.

"But, Artie," yelled Gabriel!

"Well, boys, sorry is just not going to cut it. I'm going to have to call the authorities," said the shopkeeper sternly.

"Just pay him, Artie! What are you doing," cried Gabriel?

Artie had no intention of paying the man. He easily had the credit to pay the man, but he didn't want the word getting out that a Highland was hanging out in uptown. The shopkeeper went into his shop to call the authorities, and Arthur yelled, "RUN GABE, RUN!!!" Gabriel hesitated but ran right after Arthur. They ran around the street corner to where the car was parked and got into the car. They told the driver to get out of there fast. The driver didn't question. By the time the two shopkeepers realized what had happened, the two boys were out of sight.

"What the HELL, Artie," yelled Gabriel.

"Look, the one place I can go and be just a kid is in that place," said Arthur. "If word gets out a Highland child is hanging out and flaunting money in uptown, I may never get to go back again. The people of the uptown like their place, they don't like us midtowners coming in and showing off, especially kids."

"Well, I'd say we can never go back to that shop again. I liked that bike. It was fun, Artie," said Gabriel.

"There are plenty of bike shops in the metropolis, and besides wasn't that exhilarating, running from that man," said Arthur with a sly grin and dismissive demeanor.

"No, no, it wasn't. Don't ever do that to me again. Artie, we just ruined that man's bike," said Gabriel.

"No, actually, you just ruined that man's bike," said Arthur laughing. "Look, Gabe, I'm sorry I promise I'll never do that again. I swear. Look, let's forget about that now Gabe, look at your arm, it's all bloody."

"It doesn't hurt," said Gabriel looking at his arm and holding the scrape.

"You're not gonna pout, are you Gabe," asked Arthur? "Let's just go home, and Angela can tend to you. You're not mad, are you Gabe? I'm really sorry. Let's just enjoy the rest of the night, okay?"

"Okay, but don't ever do that again," said Gabriel.

The boys shared a car ride of silence. Gabriel saw a side of Arthur that he had never seen, that spoiled little brat he had a feeling was there. Perhaps this was the very reason Mr. Highland had accepted him into the family, to rid Arthur of his imperfections of flagrant excess and absurdity. Perhaps these were the very actions that Mr. Highland wanted Gabriel to exorcise out of his son.

The boys arrived home just after dark, through the revolving door and through Clarence's watch on the elevator, and up to the penthouse. James opened the door, and Angela came wondering where the boys had been. She saw his elbow and ran him straight to the back bathroom, ran the scrape under some water to clean it. Gabriel pulled his arm back because it stung a little bit, but she continued anyway. When she was done washing his arm, she doctored it with peroxide and eventually put a large bandage over it. "It shouldn't scar Gabriel, dear boy," she said. The boys went to their room until dinner was served.

"Please don't tell my father about what happened today Gabe, he'd never let us out like that again," said Arthur. "I know it was irresponsible, but I was just trying to have some fun. But hey! You really liked that bike, didn't you, though?"

"Yeah, but you ruined all chance of me getting it," said Gabriel turning away from Arthur.

"Don't be so sure of that, Gabe," said Arthur. "Let's just forget this happened and have a good dinner, tomorrow we'll walk around midtown, we probably shouldn't go to uptown for a while. I think we're having filet mignon tonight, garlic mashed potatoes, and asparagus, my second favorite meal. What do you say, let's go help, Angela?"

"Fine then, we'll just tell your parents we were wrestling at the park," said Gabriel.

"Great! That's the spirit. Come on!"

The boys made it to the kitchen to help Angela. Arthur was accustomed to mashing the potatoes, but he felt it better to let Gabriel in lieu of the circumstances. Gabriel recalled doing much of the same thing while he was at home. He also thought that his father would have never let him get away with what had happened that day. Gabriel tried to forget, but it just kept coming back. He thought Mr. Highland needed him to make his son a more well-rounded person. He would do just that, help keep Arthur in line.

Dinner came and went, the Highlands asking what happened, and as a best friend would he told them, they were wrestling. After the meal, the two boys went to their room, full and content, Gabriel feeling better felt the necessity to beg questions. "Artie, what's your first memory?"

Artie thought for a moment and remembered a certain evening, the farthest back he could remember. "I can remember going to bed when the sun was still up, my mother put me to bed, and I can recall seeing shapes on the ceiling, they were moving like little animals. It turns out I had a mobile of animals over my bed until I was about four. So, I really don't know how old I was, but that's around the first memories I have. I can also remember a very faint image of my grandfather, sitting on his lap. I had a cowboy hat on, and we were playing like cowboys. I think that's it, but that was a long time ago. What about you, Gabe?"

Gabriel pondered a moment and thought maybe he shouldn't share these memories because he didn't need them anymore. But he said, "It's not so much a specific memory like yours, it's really a recurring memory."

"Well, what is it," asked Arthur?

"I can remember watching my mom so many times hanging the laundry out on the line. I probably was barely four. I know it was only about two and a half years ago, but that just always flashes through my mind, her in her white spring dress. I know I shouldn't want that, but I feel like I don't understand some of the things you do. So much frivolity and excess, my parents were simple people."

"We're simple people, Gabe," added Arthur. "If you're still thinking about today, maybe I was just showing off a little. I think we're the same, we just come from different places. Maybe today, I wanted to know if you would run when I ran, maybe I needed to know you trusted me. I've never had a friend before, Gabe. I've had some kids I knew from school, but don't you see why my father allowed you into our family? I almost wanted you to stop me from running today, though. It's like I'm immortal because of who my father is. Gabe, I see you teaching me and me teaching you, that's at least what I hope for."

"What do I have to teach you, though," asked Gabriel?

"That I'm not an immortal. Think about it, you come from the outer parts, and I come from the midtown district. Just maybe we can make a pact to meet in the middle in the uptown part of town. Maybe as men, we'll live in the middle, neither of us better, neither of us lesser than the other, both equal in our relationship. Let's just say when we're out of school we're going to be best friends still. Will you swear on it, Gabe?"

"On one condition," he said.

"Okay, one condition."

"Tomorrow, you'll mail the money for that bike with an anonymous apology letter to that shopkeeper. Tell him you had the money you just got scared, you hope he isn't too cross, and that if he ever sees us again not to call the cops. That's what an honest man would do, Artie. I can't say what a rich man would do because I'm not one. That's my condition, do you agree?"

"I believe I have learned my first lesson from you, Gabe, honesty," said Arthur. "I'll agree, Gabriel Liden, and we'll call it our first lesson. We'll call it the honorable cyclist's lesson, for you are honorable, but I can't say you're much of a cyclist, at least not yet."

"Then I swear we'll meet in the middle," said Gabriel.

The middle Gabriel...

Chapter 4

The Middle

The two boys went to sleep that night in hopes of getting proper rest. They knew that each would indeed learn from one another, thus fulfilling their pact. Gabriel thought to himself, well after Arthur had fallen asleep, that maybe he had a problem as well. Perhaps, because he felt it was so challenging to go from the outer parts to the upper echelon in his mind. The middle was attainable, but that is not what his father had wanted for him. He looked around the room, and out the window to a full moon in December, and thought, I don't care what my father wants for me. I'm my own man now; I have a plan. Mr. Highland believes that I should forge a path of forgiveness. Well then, I forgive my mother for not knowing, but my father just wanted a rich son. Indeed, I am rich without my father, and that is how it shall stay. So Gabriel decided two things that night; he would forge on in his new life and make it the best that he could. Also, he would move on as a man of the city with goals of comfort and not of excess.

The boys woke that next morning to that somewhat familiar buzzer and crept into their bathroom. They brushed their teeth, took turns taking showers, and dressed for the cold day ahead; Gabriel even wore some of his new clothing. They met Bethany in a cleaning frenzy in the hallway and said hello. The two made their way into the breakfast nook where Angela had prepared an excellent breakfast for them. The boys seemed to brighten up as the meal went onward. “What are we going to do today, Artie?” asked Gabriel.

“First, I have a note to send to an unnamed place, then I thought we’d go just walk around.”

“Sounds good. Let’s get going,” said Gabriel. “Thank you, Angela, we’ll see you at dinner.”

“Okay, boys,” said Angela beginning to gather all of the empty plates and condiments. “Now, you two be safe. I don’t want any more scratches, you hear?”

The boys meandered towards the door and called the elevator. In a few moments, the elevator door opened. A young man opened the gate. “Hello, Mr. Highland,” said the man in the elevator.

“Hello, Claude,” said Arthur putting on his hat and gloves.

“Where’s Clarence?” asked Gabriel, a little disappointed it wasn't the silent Mr. Clarence.

“Oh, Gabriel, this is Claude. He works the other shift on the elevator,”

“Glad to meet you, Gabriel. The name is Claude Jenkins, of the southwestern metropolis Jenkins.”

“So, you’re not one of us?” asked Gabriel.

“Actually, I’m not, Mr. Gabriel. I’m sympathetic, but I am a student at Uptown University, and I am from the southwestern metropolis. I worked at one of Mr. Highland’s other hotels as bellhop since I was, oh, fifteen or so.”

“Well, how old are you now,” asked Gabriel as they stood outside the elevator?

“I’m a youthful twenty-three. You know, I have to work my way through school, so it takes longer,” he said.

"Well, Claude, I'm glad to meet you," said Gabriel. "Can you take us to the first floor, my good friend?"

"Step right in and watch me close the magic gate. Come on in, boys! Let's go for a ride!"

The boys stepped into the elevator, and the magic gate closed. Claude pulled the giant brass lever, and off they were. They made it in only a few moments down to the first floor and bid Claude a good day. The boys started down the street with no particular place to go. Long coats and black merino hats atop, they didn't say anything for a while, they just walked. Gabriel thought about his new life while Arthur pondered about what to say in his anonymous letter. After a brisk walk, the two boys came to the postal office and entered into the warm stale environment that was the postal office. Arthur had grabbed a sheet of paper and a pen before they left that morning. He began writing a short letter of apology to the shopkeeper and enclosed two hundred dollars. Gabriel asked why he put in two hundred when it was only one fifty? Arthur just replied because I can. Arthur explained that he really meant that he would keep the pact they made the night before. That philanthropy was only another branch of the same tree from which honesty stemmed. Gabriel thought for a moment, and in the end, agreed with Arthur's kind gesture.

It was early, and the shops were just beginning to open. Gabriel was interested in some of the shops, but mainly he was interested in the art venues. The Museum of Fine Arts opened at ten-thirty. The boys made a direct line for the gallery, down Main Street, and to the Metropolis Commons area. The museum was located in the center of the Commons. They arrived at the museum just as the doors were opening. They purchased two tickets that were only ten dollars, instead of fifteen, since Mr. Highland was a valued guest of the museum. They entered the line to the elevator, which would take them to the exhibits;

only two families stood in front of them. Surely, they could all fit on the elevator.

In just a few minutes, the boys started to enter the elevator. Gabriel was fascinated when they entered; there was no one operating the controls. "Arthur, how does this massive thing work without someone at the controls?" The two families snickered at the young boy.

Arthur replied, "See Gabe, the elevator you see in my father's hotel is for a show, most elevators are run by machines now, not men."

"Well, I like Clarence, even though he doesn't say anything, and of course I like Claude. They give a sense of taste and personal touch to the idea of the elevator," said Gabriel looking seemingly embarrassed at his naive remark.

Arthur explained that when elevators first came to be, they were all like the one in his father's hotel, but some ingenious men found a way to make them run by themselves. After a short ride, the elevator they were in opened to the basement floor, and the boys and the families stepped out. They were met by a tapestry explaining the purpose of the exhibit.

The exhibit that was at the museum was to showcase all the great works of art throughout history. The tapestry stated that one piece dated over three thousand years old and the newest by an impressionist. Gabriel had seen a lot of the works in socialization class, but he never thought he was going to get to see most of them in the same venue. Gabriel could not wait to see the exhibits, so they moved on.

They rounded the corner to where paintings were hung magnificently on the wall. They walked down the corridor and Gabriel was awestruck by one painting. The tapestry next to the painting told of its history:

Two hundred years ago, the artist captured the essence of the ocean in this oil on canvas painting, standing a staggering fifteen by twelve feet. The picture was the rendering of a ship lost at sea during a great storm. The piece was owned privately until the painting was placed on auction and purchased by the Halt Museum early in the current century.

Gabriel thought of these people as geniuses. However, the boy moved continued down the corridor. They came to the piece that the first tapestry had told of as being approximately three thousand years old. It was a sculpture of marble of two people entwined in a kiss. The sculpture stood as a testament to time and human nature. What Gabriel could not understand was how these people of the metropolis could appreciate such works when they were most likely the product of the people from the outer parts. The concept of the metropolis had only been around since the industrialization age. Before then, there were just towns, states, and provinces. For instance, Gabriel did not see why the very people that put down his roots in the outer parts could appreciate such ancient artistry. They knew that they admired the peace and tranquility these paintings brought them. He found the hypocrisy to be somewhat unnerving. Still, he remembered that sign in the window in uptown, the one in the outfitters, tours of the outer parts mountains, and he began to think maybe it was only the minority who hated the outer parts. "Arthur," said Gabriel, "do all the people in the metropolises hate the outer parts?"

"No, some enjoy going out of the city," said Arthur. "Some enjoy the sea while others enjoy the mountains."

"What about the country," asked Gabriel?

"The country is different than the farmlands and such. There is beauty in the sea, and there is a feeling you get when you go to the mountains, but there is nothing beautiful about the farms. That is what people really mean by the outer parts, the country."

"So, if I were from the sea it would be different," asked Gabriel?

"Well yes and no," explained Arthur. "Yes, because people from the metropolis do find the sea intriguing and beautiful, but not because well, the people of the metropolis just think their way of life is better than any of the parts of the outer parts. When you're from the sea, you most likely catch your own food, the mountaineers kill their own game, and the people from the country grow their own crops. The people of the metropolis just think it better to have someone do it for them. They don't want to tend crops or slaughter animals. They just want to live and have a good time. So, when I said we were simple people, I kind of meant lazy. Simple, because everything is done for us. In the same right, lazy because we want everything done for us. My father recognizes that the people from the outer parts are better laborers, but the people from the metropolis are better thinkers. Your father dreamed you to be a thinker, not a laborer, that's why he brought you here."

"But what if I want to be a laborer," asked Gabriel looking at a nearby painting?

"We've agreed to meet in the middle right," said Arthur. "So, when we get to the middle, when we're older, we'll have to work our minds harder if that's what you want. That doesn't mean our bodies, but for now, let's enjoy being young thinkers and think about how good we have it. It may not always be this way. My father could lose his fortune, or just think, the school could have turned you away, but they didn't. So, here's my first lesson to you, Gabe. Enjoy what you have; enjoy the moment. Right now, you're in the presence of most of the great works of art in history, and all you're worried about is whether they respect these artists because most of them are from the outer parts. Come on, man, live a little. Remember, we aim for the middle now. That means you're not poor and I'm not rich, we're just here together. Now, the fact that we have the money to be here is another thing. Let's just go through today and enjoy seeing these things together; we may never see them like this again."

"I understand, Artie. Let's just enjoy the day."

The two boys did as they said they would. They walked through the museum enjoying the works of art, whether the artist was from the outer parts or a far metropolis. They stopped by the museum gift shop on the way out after another ride in the odd unmanned elevator and bought a calendar showcasing the exhibits. They also purchased a set of colored pencils with the museum's name on them. Then the two-headed back out into the streets once more.

They went to Lordes and walked around, this time Gabriel getting to go to the sports department and look at all the sports memorabilia. Gabriel asked Artie if he would buy him a Metro's basketball jersey, and then it hit Arthur, perhaps they should go to a game. Arthur asked the salesman in the department if he knew if there was a Metro's game tonight, and wouldn't you know it, there was. Gabriel was overcome with anticipation. The boys used the phone in the store to call home and relay to James that they would not be home for the dinner hour; they would be at the game.

The boys waited out the rest of the day, ducking in shops and occasionally stopping to get a bite to eat. Those few hours passed between the department store and the time for the game. The boys made their way in a cab to the heart of the city. They got out of the cab and began walking down the street to where the box office was located. The streets were filled with over-zealous fanatics for both sides. The two were approached by several ticket scalpers on the way in, but Arthur knew he could get a better seat at the box office. He knew his father had courtside season tickets; he had been with his father several times in the last few years.

Gabriel, wearing his new jersey, followed Arthur in wonder around the area, for the arena was quite a sight, not just for

Gabriel, but for anyone. It was located near a transit station, next to the news station; it was among the towering skyscrapers of the heart of the city. They eventually made it to the ticket office and went to the window labeled season ticket holders. Arthur explained who he was, asked for the tickets, and they were given their courtside ticket stubs, and they were on their way.

They entered through the main entrance, through the turnstiles, and into the crowd of festive fans. They made it to the gate, E 3, walked down the steep steps, and found their seats. Gabriel was amazed at all the people, for he had never seen so many people at one time. He and Arthur settled into their prime seating, just taking in the air of the arena.

"Popcorn, Dogs, Peanuts, Beer, Cola" came from a nearby vendor as they sat waiting for the game to start.

Arthur yelled, "Two dogs and two colas! Oh, and why not some peanuts, we're living in the moment tonight, right?"

"Right," yelled Gabriel in excitement!

The game started with the tip-off promptly at eight o'clock, and Gabriel was struck speechless by the sheer size of the men of the Metro's; one man was near seven feet five inches tall. Gabriel's frame of reference was not very good for the tallest man he had probably ever seen was only about six foot four, a neighbor of his in the outer parts. Nonetheless, the men looked like giants.

The game progressed, and the Metros were well ahead of the northeast metropolitan Stars at halftime. The boys got out of their seats and made a quick break for the restrooms before the crowd hit. Gabriel entered the restroom and was taken aback, for what he saw he couldn't explain; he didn't know what to do. He thought it looked like a trough-like back at home, but why was it in the restroom. Arthur laughed and said, "It's a urinal Gabe; you go to the bathroom in it."

"It looks like a trough from back home the animals used," he laughed.

"I guess we're animals then," laughed Arthur.

The boys urinated for what seemed to be minutes and then buttoned themselves and headed back to their seats. The second half of the game started, and it was definitely a show for the young men. The Metros were in the running for first place with the Stars, so it was a heated battle of a game. Dunk after dunk, steal after steal, and shot after shot, the boys stood and cheered for their home team. The Stars battled hard against the Metro's, but in the end, the Metros were too much for them.

The score was 101 to 97 at the end of the game in favor of the Metros. The boys got up and made their way up the stairs and out of the arena. They hailed a cab and headed for the midtown district; Gabriel was still excited about the process of a professional game. They arrived home at eleven fifteen, up the elevator with Clarence and into the small hallway of the penthouse floor. Once again, Arthur fumbled for his key but was met by James at the door.

"Aren't you boys home a little late? Your father and mother were worried," said James.

"We called earlier. Don't you remember? Besides, we were at the Metros game," said Arthur in their defense.

"Game or not, you boys should try to go to bed," said James taking their coats and hats.

The boys made it inside the door and through the living room towards their bedroom. Angela poked her head from around the corner and said, "Do you boys need any food, I was about to go to bed?"

"No, thank you," said the boys. They thanked Angela and headed straight for their room.

After a few moments the boys had readied themselves for bed, but Mr. Highland came around the corner and walked in the room and said, "Did you boys have a good time, James said you went to the game, I was watching it on television."

Gabriel blurted out, "Arthur bought me a jersey, and we got to see the whole game."

"Whose jersey did you buy? I take it, you two went to Lordes today," said Mr. Highland.

"I got the big guy's jersey Haw: number 23," said Gabriel.

"Yeah, dad, we had a great time, we used the season tickets. Did you see us on TV," asked Arthur?

"I didn't see you two, but I'm sure you had a great time. Now I think you two should go to sleep, young men need their rest so they can play hard," said Mr. Highland, "Now off you go."

"Goodnight, Dad," said Arthur.

"Goodnight, Haw," said Gabriel.

"Night, boys," said Mr. Highland. "By-the-way boys, I have to go to one of the other hotels for the next few days. Your mother and I will be flying out tomorrow. James will be in charge, so no fooling around."

The boys went to sleep again that night. Gabriel was still excited about the game. Arthur was happy he could teach his best friend a life lesson, one that he thought to be profound. The next few days came and went, the boys doing similar things during the day, but spending some quality time with James and Angela. Bethany was there during the days but went home at night. Gabriel still had his schoolboy crush. They had fine-cooked meals with the best produce and the best meats the metropolis had to offer. Gabriel was right at home after that first week of introduction to his new life. The boys were once again thick as thieves. They played as children but learned like men.

After those few days, Mr. and Mrs. Highland came home, and the boy's daily routine didn't change much. They got up and wandered the city, ate, and slept. It was the holiday season, and after all, the Highlands loved the holiday season. Arthur and Gabriel went shopping at Lordes for Arthur's parents and found unique gifts for the rest of the household. Gabriel tried to pick out things that the family would remember, not necessarily things that cost a lot or were flashy.

The night before, the grand holiday of the believers came, and the boys made the most of it. In the Highland tradition, the tree was put up the morning before the holiday. Angela, James, and Bethany, and the boys all worked tirelessly that morning, stringing lights and hanging garland. It was a grand tree, almost ten feet tall, as wide as their grand hallway. It made the home look comfortable among what Gabriel thought to be odd décor. Eventually, around twelve o'clock, the loving help and the boys had put up the tree, strung the lights, and hung the garland. The house was very festive, and the boys thought it now okay to do the last-minute things they had to do. The shopping was done, except for one last thing to find. Gabriel and Arthur wandered the streets trying to find a last-minute gift for Bethany, one she would not forget. Gabriel suggested they go to the uptown district, much to Arthur's surprise, to look and find something there. Arthur thought it might be a good idea, so they went back to the hotel and commandeered the Highland's personal driver. They made their way to Virginia Avenue.

They arrived at around three-thirty in the afternoon. The two didn't have much time because they knew all the shops would close at six, for most of the metropolis celebrated the grand holiday. They combed all the local shops and an hour passed. But suddenly, Gabriel had an idea. He remembered Bethany saying she was from the outer parts of the mountains. So, he went to the outdoor outfitters and offered them one hundred dollars for the sign saying tours of the outer parts in the mountains. It was perfect, he thought. Arthur just laughed at his school-boy crush but gave great applause for his attention to detail. She would love it, they thought, but he would have to give it to her in private, or Mr. Highland would surely figure out where they'd been.

They headed back to the limousine and started back toward the Metropolitan Plaza; it was five forty-five. They knew they had to be back and dressed for a seven o'clock dinner with the family, but rush hour was still raging. All those that could not afford to take a great deal of time off were hurriedly making their way home. The boys knew they were pressed for time, but they just had to wait.

Eventually, traffic died just, and they made it home at six forty-five. The two ran through the revolving door and to the elevator. They told Clarence to make it quick; they had dinner to make. He closed the brass door and throttled the handle, and off they went. They made it in no time. James was waiting at the front door for them. They went into the house, and Angela told them they'd better make it quick. No time for showering, just a change of clothes while Angela wrapped their gifts in a hurry. Not unlike a lot of families, the Highland's opened one present the night before the grand holiday, but Gabriel wondered which one he would open.

Dinner was a grand affair; Angela had outdone herself. There was turkey, dressing, peas, and plenty of conversation to hold the meal together. Mr. Highland discussed his plans for the coming school year. He told of some new curriculum changes, while Mrs. Highland told of her sister's new home in the far seas metropolis. The boys ate aplenty and were thankful for a glorious meal. Mr. Highland leaned over and whispered to Gabriel that he had something for him in private. Gabriel wondered what he could have. "Boys! Your grades came in, but whose shall I tell first. Gabriel, you are the guest, Arthur is my son, so we'll flip a coin. Heads or tails, Gabriel," asked Mr. Highland?

"I'll take heads, Haw," said Gabriel as he sat up and readied himself for the toss.

"Then heads you shall have Gabriel," said Mr. Highland playfully throwing and catching the coin.

Haw flipped the coin, caught it, and slapped it on the outside of his left hand, covering it with his right hand. He paused for a moment making the boys squirm just a little bit. "Come on, father," yelled Arthur in anticipation!

"Yeah, let's have it, Haw," yelled Gabriel!

Mr. Highland took a look under his right hand and said, "I wonder who it will be, Mr. Gabriel or Mr. Arthur?"

"Enough, father," said Arthur excitedly!

"Very well, Arthur, you win: its tales," said Mr. Highland. "Arthur, you made four A's and two B's, not too shabby. Gabriel, the surprise of the year! You earned beautiful marks not only for your first semester but for anyone. All A's Gabriel, congratulations. Especially to be noted, Gabriel. You made three A-pluses: one in English; one in Physical Education, and one in Socialization."

Arthur gave a yell in tribute to his best friend, "You've achieved so much Gabe, congratulations!"

Arthur had genuine respect for Gabriel, and knowing his marks only strengthened that respect. Mr. Highland said to the boys, "Dinner is through, now we all shall gather around the tree for the gift of one's choice."

The boys made their way into the living room, where the grand tree was displayed in all its grandeur. "Go ahead and pick," said Mr. Highland as the boys perused the gifts on the floor. Arthur located Angela's present right off the bat while Gabriel searched a little bit closer. He had not had much contact with Mrs. Highland, so he looked for her present to him and grabbed it. It was not a large gift, only a small box. "Interesting choice Gabriel. Remember I told you I had something to tell you. Well, what I wanted to tell you is in that box," said Mr. Highland. The others found their gifts and readied themselves for the reveal.

Mrs. Highland said to Gabriel, "I thought you needed this gift, so take it for what it's worth."

Everyone dug into the wrapping paper, and each was revealed a present. Mr. Highland chose Arthur's gift, which was a Metro's jersey, much like the one Gabriel had. Angela chose James, and Bethany chose Mr. Highland. They all received wonderful gifts from each other, but Gabriel was puzzled by what he found when he opened his small box. There was a letter with a postal marking and the address of the school and a return address, bearing the name of Anne Liden. Gabriel didn't know what to think. He wandered off into the kitchen and opened the letter; it read as such:

Dear Gabriel,

I don't know if you'll get this letter by the great holiday or at all for that matter. Your father, Liza, and I miss you a lot. It just hasn't been the same since you left. I know you're probably hurt right now, but in time I hope you'll come to remember that we love you dearly. The school will allow us to visit come the first of next year. I hope you'll receive us. Wherever you are, I know you're thinking of us, and I hope you're in good hands. I look forward to seeing you in a few months, and please write if you can.

Love,

Mama

At first, Gabriel lamented and thought deeply about the letter, but then he remembered they left him and what he had resigned himself to do. He walked back into the living room, and the family was waiting, Mrs. Highland had told them what was in the box. Mrs. Highland said, "It is a time to rejoice, and I hope whatever it said made you feel like rejoicing."

Gabriel didn't think the news was grand. He remembered, however, that his new family was there for him and that he was a lucky man. Arthur said to live in the moment, so that is what he would do. He swallowed his pride and said, "The letter was positive, and all is well with my family; let us rejoice now."

The family knew that Gabriel was probably hurting a little inside. After all, it's not easy being taken from your family and replaced by a surrogate one. Mr. Highland knew he would give him a good life, so all was well. "Gabriel! Arthur! Come give your father a hug and then make your way to sleep, the holiday keeper will be here soon. Go now, boys, sleep."

The boys finished their hug, Gabriel holding on a little longer and then releasing so he could follow Arthur to bed. Angela followed to tuck the boys in for the night. They brushed their teeth and changed into their bedtime clothes and crawled into bed. Gabriel said to Arthur, "What do you think the holiday keeper will give you this year."

"Please tell me you don't really believe in the holiday keeper," said Arthur sitting up in his bed and throwing the covers to his waist.

"Why would I not, Artie?"

"Arthur, if Gabriel believes in the holiday keeper, perhaps you should believe in him as well," said Angela tucking Gabriel into his bed.

"I don't believe in such nonsense," said Arthur. "When I was four years old, I saw my parents bringing the gifts that the holiday keeper supposedly brought. Gabe, there is no holiday keeper. It's been a year of surprises, what's one more, right."

"I believe you, Arthur, but why would they have told us that lie," asked Gabriel?

Angela chimed in and said, "Because they love you."

"They love you, yeah," said Arthur. "But kids like you and me are smarter than most, we think like adults, not children. So why would you want to live the lies of a child."

"I guess I wouldn't," said Gabriel with a deep sigh.

Angela told them to rest and have a great night's sleep, holiday keeper, or not; they would have a glorious morning. The boys pulled their covers up and headed to sleep, Gabriel was tired of surprises. The Highland's moved the gifts out as soon as they thought the boys were asleep and headed to sleep themselves. Angela and James turned off the lights and retired around eleven-thirty that night, for the great holiday always came soon after sunrise; they needed to be rested.

The boys woke this time, not to the buzzer, but the thrill of excitement and the wonder of youth. The boys got out of bed and made their way into the living room; Mr. Highland was waiting for them. "Boys! Come see what the holiday keeper brought you."

Arthur looked at his father and said, "We know there's no holiday keeper father, you can drop the act."

"What do you mean, no holiday keeper boys, of course there's a holiday keeper," said Mr. Highland. He motioned to the boys and whispered, "Your mother still thinks you believe, so just play along. What do you say, guys?"

The boys agreed to play along for Arthur's mother's sake, and a few moments later, Mrs. Highland came out of the kitchen, saying, "Boys, boys, boys! Come look at what the keeper brought you." She ran into the living room and started handing out presents, James and Angela watched on just as Bethany knocked on the door. "James, can you get that please?" said Mrs. Highland. "Hello, Bethany. You're just in time, come, come."

Bethany, James, and Angela came to the living room as did the boys and Mr. Highland. They all started ripping into presents, revealing to the adults, and the boys, what the keeper had brought them. Gabriel went through his gifts slowly because he and his sister used to have a contest to see who would have the last present.

A good forty minutes passed, and Gabriel wondered at all his gifts, Mr. Highland had opened him a bank account and filled it with five thousand dollars, Angela had made him a scarf with the colors of the Highland family crest and even placed his initials on the ends. James was a little less sentimental with a poster of the colossal painting he had seen at the museum. Arthur tipped him off. He had already received Mrs. Highlands, but he had not received one from Bethany or Arthur. In a joking manner, Gabriel said, "Bethany, do you not love me?"

Bethany walked across the room and said, "I couldn't think of what to get you, so I thought I'd get you this." Bethany walked across the room and gave Gabriel a kiss on the cheek, and the boy began to blush. The family just laughed as Gabriel shied away and said, "So, you do love me."

"I love to embarrass you, Gabriel, that's all," said Bethany. "Welcome to the family and happy great holiday, Gabe."

"You called me Gabe."

"Don't let it go to your head, little one. Besides, I've already got a boyfriend, sorry," said Bethany stroking her hair comically like a child.

Everyone had a good laugh, everyone but Gabriel had opened all of their gifts, he thought to himself, "Yes, I won." But then he remembered his gift to Bethany, that would have to wait until later he thought, no need to stir things with Mr. Highland.

"Now you're probably wondering Gabe where my present is," said Arthur.

"I didn't expect anything, Artie," said Gabriel.

"But that's not the Highland way. I thought long and hard about what to get you. I know you like sports and stuff like that, but there's something you want, but you don't even know you want it. Your eyes have seldom sparkled as when you saw this gift. James, can you get the gift," asked Arthur.

James went to one of the back rooms, one where Gabriel had not been, and came out with the very item that started their pact, Gabriel could not believe his eyes. "You got me a bicycle. Artie, thank you, thank you, thank you!!!"

"My father had a little bit to do with it, too," said Arthur looking extremely satisfied with himself.

"Can we try it out, please? Come on, guys!"

Gabriel headed for the door along with Arthur and the rest of the family. "We can't all fit in the elevator with the bicycle," said Mr. Highland.

"Well then... Arthur, Haw, and Angela let's go," said Gabriel.

The others stayed behind, and the foursome headed out the door. They called the elevator, and in a moment, the door opened up, and Claude greeted them, saying, "Happy great holiday to you, folks. Where are we going at such an hour? Oh, never mind! Whose bike?"

"Mine! Now hurry, Claude," said Gabriel.

They got in the elevator and closed the brass gate, and Claude said, "Hold on! The bullet train's going down kids!" They passed the other guests calling the elevator and went straight to the lobby, Gabriel exploding with excitement. They ran from the elevator past the ballrooms and by the front desk. The only problem now was how to get the bike out of the revolving door. Gabriel sized it up, "Yeah, it'll fit if I stand it up. "And he did just that. He made it through the door with little to no problems, but now he was on the outside in his bedclothes cheeks beginning to redden, nose beginning to chill. "Last time I did this, I wrecked, but I'll remember the brakes this time," said Gabriel.

Arthur was kind enough to have fitted it with training wheels, for he knew it would take a while for him to break free. Gabriel adjusted the seat, sat down, and began pushing on the pedals. "I'm moving," he cried as he started rounding the cobblestone roundabout.

"Use the brakes, son," said Mr. Highland.

Gabriel hit them hard at first then pedaled again, braking and pedaling, continuing this for a few minutes around the roundabout. He eventually got the hang of it. Arthur looked on as his best friend had a glow about him and a lust for life; he was happy. "Come on in now, boy. You're going to freeze out there, we can ride later," said Mr. Highland.

Gabriel and the extended Highland family enjoyed the rest of the morning and on into the evening. They all rejoiced in the great holiday and were thankful for one another, and they all retired around the hour of eleven. Gabriel and Arthur thanked each other for their gifts and Arthur teased Gabriel about his kiss on the cheek, Gabriel laughed. They went to sleep happy to be together and slept as though they had never slept.

The morning came, but the boys chose to sleep in and enjoy a morning of good rest rather than having an adventure. They eventually woke, and Angela fixed them some food. They headed out to the streets to ride their bicycles. The day just seemed to get away from them, Gabriel eventually getting brave enough to take the training wheels off. He crashed a few times but soon got the hang of it. And that's how the next few days went, the boys riding their bikes all over the midtown district. One day they even got up early and ventured to the uptown district even going to the bike shop to make amends. The shopkeeper was kind but firm with the boys. Gabriel, with his new bank account, spent some money on new brakes and some reflectors for his wheels.

Eventually, the new year came, and the family gathered in the heart of the city to watch the grand fireworks show. Gabriel had never seen them before. The midnight hour came and went, and the family made it home to crawl into bed at the late hour of two in the morning. That was the latest night the boys had ever seen. New year's day was quiet in midtown and even uptown, and all enjoyed that day of the year off. Gabriel and Arthur walked the quiet streets just laughing and recalling all they had done. School started in two days, and they were trying to make the best of it. They spent the day before school riding around the city. They even ventured to the heart of uptown, just to look at all the buildings in their magnificence.

The next semester eventually came, and the first semester of socialization, history, English, mathematics, and science was behind them. The boys returned that Sunday to their dorm room, readying themselves for the beginning of another grueling semester. During the middle of the day, the boys managed to escape the school grounds and bike around the seedy area that was downtown. They made it back before nightfall, for they did not dare brave the streets of downtown after dark. Mr. Highland stopped in to wish the boys good luck for that semester and headed back to the hotel to be with Mrs. Highland. The two boys laughed but prepared themselves for the upcoming classes and eventually made their way towards the bed. Gabriel would attend socialization class in the morning followed by science class, and Arthur beginning the day with physical education and on to mathematics; both would meet for the eleven o'clock lunch hour. But those classes were still a dream away for the boys, sleep would come easy for them that night, and those dreams were of bliss. Goodnight Boys...

Chapter 5

On the Move

The semester at The Highland Boys School began as any would. There was a hustle-and-bustle with socialization class with Mr. Riley, but all they really did was discuss his interaction with the Highland family, and the rest of the city. He told of his visit to the museum and his bicycle debacle, changing the story a little to protect himself and Arthur. He went to his science class and mathematics as he would have done the semester before. Not too much changed, in fact not much changed the rest of that year. Gabriel did, however, take the time to write his mother; he said that he was content. He hoped the same for them, and that he was satisfied with his resolution.

He and Arthur were the best of friends, and nothing could break their pact. Occasionally, they would go riding through the city now that the days were longer, and light allowed for more exploration. Some time went by, and Gabriel never received a letter back from his mother. It was something that seemed to bother him a little. Mr. Highland was supportive of both Arthur and Gabriel throughout the year. Eventually, the semester ended. There was a month and a half break for the boys until the next year would begin, of course, they went to the Highland residence for the duration.

A few weeks went by and the boy's grades made it to the penthouse. Gabriel and Arthur received similar marks as the semester before. They were both were satisfied with their marks and then forged on into the summer. It was a sultry summer in the metropolis that year. Gabriel was a still little lost, considering his mother still had not written him back. They had plans to see one another the day before the new school year began. He was reluctant yet strangely hopeful to see them. Nonetheless, he forged on, riding through the city with Arthur on his new bicycle, using the money Mr. Highland had given him wisely.

Eventually, the long, hot, and humid summer came to an end. The boys went back to school two days early, for they didn't know whether Gabriel would be meeting his mother and father or not. The previous day to school began and Gabriel expected to at least hear from his parents. He went to Mr. Riley's office and waited that morning. His father was supposedly delivering his crops on that day. Gabriel waited that morning, anxious to see his parents. The morning crept by and then eventually into the daytime. Gabriel often got up and stood at the window a few times and looked out, hoping to see his mother and father. The minutes were agonizing, for he did and did not want to see them. Somewhere in his heart, he knew something was not right. Suddenly, out the window, the boy saw his father's truck. The headmaster came out onto the cobblestone driveway and met Mr. Liden. They seemed to talk for a few minutes, and then Mr. Liden got back into his truck and began turning around. Gabriel ran frantically out of the building to try and catch a brief moment with his father, but he drove off quite in a hurry.

The headmaster was still standing out on the cobblestone when Gabriel reached the spot where they were talking. The headmaster turned to Gabriel and said, "Your father will no longer be paying for your school. He is unable to fulfill his end of our bargain."

"What does this mean, headmaster," asked Gabriel?

"It means you no longer go here, boy. So pack your things and ready yourself for leaving, you have one hour."

Gabriel ran immediately to Mr. Riley's office and made a frantic call to Mr. Highland. He answered the call and Gabriel said, "Haw, they've kicked me out of school. The headmaster said my father couldn't hold up his end of the bargain. What bargain?"

"Now calm down, Gabriel. We can get this worked out. I'm on the board of trustees, remember. Now your father had agreed to pay for your school by bartering crops for your education. Something may have gone wrong with his crops. He may not have been able to fulfill his obligation. Gabriel, I'm going to hang up the phone, call the headmaster and the board members, and get this straightened out. I'm not letting you leave this school, Gabriel, don't worry. Now, go find Arthur, and I'll call you within the hour."

Gabriel ran frantically to his dorm room, where Arthur was waiting for him. "How'd the meeting go?"

"He showed but without payment for my school. Artie, I don't know what to do. You've got to help me. Tell your father he's got to help me. I have nowhere to go, Artie, nowhere," cried Gabriel.

"I'm sure my father will get this straightened out, just calm down, you're going to give yourself a heart attack," said Arthur.

Gabriel put his head in his hands and began saying, "I hate him, Artie, I hate him. How could he do this to me?"

Arthur consoled his best friend as best he could. It was a very long forty-five minutes, but soon there was a ring on the hallway phone. Gabriel ran frantically to answer it, "Hello!"

"Gabriel, it's Haw."

"Please tell me you figured something out, Haw," cried Gabriel.

"Gabriel, you're a lucky man, you're lucky you've done so well this past year. The board has decided to grant you a full scholarship! Do you hear me, Gabriel? A full scholarship," said Mr. Highland.

Gabriel cried, "Please tell me you're not joking. Please tell me what you're saying is true."

"I told you I'd take care of things, Gabriel," said Mr. Highland. "You'll start classes just like everyone else tomorrow. Now just calm yourself down and try not to think of what happened anymore, it's over. But if you must know, the headmaster said your father's crops were bad this year. It's not that he doesn't love you, your mother too, they're just having a bad year."

"Thank you, Haw, but I don't ever want to see him again," said Gabriel.

"You don't have to if you don't want to, Gabriel," said Mr. Highland. "Just remember they've fallen on hard times. If it wasn't for your father putting you here, you too might be falling on hard times right now, too."

"Thank you, Haw, I'm eternally grateful," said Gabriel.

"Now just rest up for the day ahead, okay? We'll talk later," said Mr. Highland.

They hung up the phone, and Gabriel retired with Arthur. The situation was not necessarily what it seemed to be, however. The moment had been handled amicably by Mr. Highland, but not as had been explained earlier. The fact of the matter was that the school had not placed Gabriel on full scholarship. In fact, they had wished to kick him out. Mr. Highland had agreed to pay his room, board, and meals and to take the boy in for good, finally. That is how the boy came to stay at the school. That was the only way the headmaster and school would let him stay. Mr. Highland did not think twice when this scenario was put forth in front of him. He did for the boy what he thought was best. In the end, Mr. Highland saved the boy's life concerning his schooling, and also his relationship with his son.

The next day began for the two boys. Gabriel was feeling slightly uneasy and embarrassed, but eventually, the feelings went away as the day pressed on. That year was the first year he was free from Mr. Riley's socialization class. Gabriel saw him on campus every once and a while, even asking him if he had a new student. Mr. Riley told him he couldn't say to him if he could, but they shook hands and smiled as they passed ever so often. Gabriel was indeed proud of all that he had achieved.

He was now a full-fledged student, no longer under the new school category. He studied diligently, and his marks were near perfect, still holding a great interest in language and literature. It was a quick year for the boys. The first semester went by swiftly and without incident. Gabriel spent the holiday at the Highland's. Basically, he became the child of Ignatious Hawthorn Highland. They clothed him, they fed him, and they taught him how to be a man. The great holiday was grand for the boys; presents, food, and great company. The boys rode all through town on their bicycles that holiday. Once again, Gabriel was adding to his bike all the time, trying to be faster than Arthur. Arthur was just as good of an athlete as Gabriel, but he let him sometimes win in the straight-a-ways.

The new year came and went, and the boys headed back to school, starting yet another long semester. Before he went, he wrote a short letter to his mother. He said he was doing alright, and he hoped for a good crop this year. He wrote, knowing there would not be an answer, but it brought him comfort anyway.

The first day of school began, and Mr. Riley approached Gabriel while he was walking through the schoolyard. He asked him to join him in his office. They walked through the yard and to his office, where Gabriel sat and wondered why he was there. "Am I in trouble," asked Gabriel?

"No, no, Gabriel, you're not in trouble," said Mr. Riley, "In fact, we here at The Boys School would like you to take a placement test."

"A placement test for what Mr. Fineous," asked Gabriel?

"Well, we think you might be challenged a little more if you were in a tougher, more rigorous environment, perhaps even skipping a grade, Gabriel," said Mr. Riley.

"You mean, go to Arthur's grade and his classes," asked Gabriel?

"Yes, depending on how you do on the test. Now nothing is guaranteed, but we'd like you to just try," said Mr. Riley.

"I'll do my best, Mr. Fineous. When would you like me to take it," asked Gabriel?

"Finish out your classes today and get some rest," said Mr. Riley. "We'd like you to come in tomorrow at eight. The test takes a few hours, and we don't want you out of class for too long. So go on to your next class and rest well. Just be in my office in the morning by eight."

"Thank you, Mr. Riley! I'll take this opportunity very seriously. Thank you."

"I'll see you tomorrow, Gabriel."

Gabriel made it to his remaining classes that day and met up with Arthur. He told him of the news, and Arthur was excited about the possibility of having him in his classes. But Gabriel did as Mr. Riley has asked, and he went to bed early and got a good night's rest.

The seven o'clock hour came swiftly, and the buzzer woke both Gabriel and Arthur. Arthur pushed the snooze button, and Gabriel made his way to the showers. He readied himself physically and mentally for the exam and went to Mr. Riley's office at five 'til eight.

"Right on time, even a little early, Gabriel. Very good," said Mr. Riley. "Gabriel, I'd like you to meet Mr. Fischer. He's been assigned to give you the exam."

"Pleased to meet you, Mr. Fischer," said Gabriel looking around the room.

"Gabriel, it's a pleasure to meet such a brilliant young boy. I'm interested to see what you can do. So, what do you say we get started?"

Mr. Fischer sat Gabriel down and gave him a pencil and instructed him on how the exam would work. "It is multiple-choice," he said, "some fill in the blank, and an essay at the end. Do you have any questions?"

"Just one. How is the test evaluated," asked Gabriel?

"It's simple, Gabriel. Once you finish the exam, we will feed your score sheet into a machine for your multiple-choice, your fill-in-the-blanks and essay will be judged and evaluated by me. Are you ready now?"

"Yes, I'm ready," said Gabriel.

The test was placed in front of him, and he began. He went rather quickly through the first part of the exam and then on to fill in the blanks. A couple of hours went by, and he came to the essay portion of the exam. The essay was to be written about how he saw himself in the future. He made a breeze of the essay in under half an hour and put his pencil down.

Mr. Fischer took the exam off the table and said, "Well done, Gabriel, now you should probably make it to your next class. We'll let you know tomorrow how you did on the examination. Remember, this is just a placement exam, there is no right or wrong. It's just to help us help you a little bit more."

Gabriel left and went to his classes and finished out the day. He was a little anxious, for he really wanted to be in class with Arthur. That was a long night for Gabriel. Arthur tried to assure him he did very well, but he still felt uncertain. Mr. Fischer said there were no wrong or right answers. What if he didn't place well? He would feel like a failure, not unlike the feeling he had felt with his father. Gabriel didn't want to relive that agony. He went to bed that night and prepared himself for the day ahead.

They woke at eight like they normally would, Arthur and Gabriel moving to the showers. They dressed and were off to class at nine, Gabriel wondering when they would call him. He made it to lunchtime, where he met Arthur. They ate as they usually did. Mr. Fischer suddenly walked in and over to their table. "Gabriel, how are you doing today?"

Gabriel replied, "A little anxious, but I'm okay. How'd I do?"

"Gabriel, you did wonderfully. Arthur, would you excuse us," said Mr. Fischer.

"No, problem," said Arthur.

"Gabriel, you did so wonderfully that we'd like to offer you the chance to skip your current grade and move to the next," said Mr. Fischer. "How would you like that?"

"I think I'd like that a lot, actually," said Gabriel feeling the weight of the last few days lifting.

"We'd also like to put you in some honors classes in English and Mathematics. How does that sound, Gabriel?"

"Incredible, so I did really well," asked Gabriel?

"You did extremely well, Gabriel. You're a brilliant young man, and your family would be proud."

"Mr. Highland will be pleased."

"No, I meant your real family, Gabriel. They would be proud."

"I don't care what they think. The Highlands are my family now," said Gabriel looking down.

"If that's the way you wish to have it, Gabriel. If you ever want to talk about anything, just come to my office. We've given you and Arthur the same schedule, so you'll begin those classes tomorrow. Take the rest of the day off and go for a ride around town. Yes, we know you two sneak off, but don't worry, everything's alright."

"Thank you, Mr. Fischer. I would like a ride," said Gabriel smiling graciously.

"Go now, son, and just remember to be back before dark. It's not always that safe when the sun goes down. Would you like me to get Arthur out of his classes for the rest of the day?"

"That would be amazing, thank you," said Gabriel gathering his things from the table.

Mr. Fischer did just that. When Arthur arrived, Gabriel told him the good news, and the boys went straight to where their bicycles were and headed out the front gate. They spent the rest of the afternoon riding about town and celebrating Gabriel's triumph. Arthur assured him he would do well. They stopped to phone after a while in the middle of the afternoon to call Mr. Highland. Gabriel told him of the news, and Mr. Highland said he was as proud of him as he would be if it were Arthur.

The boys returned to school just as the sun was setting. Gabriel was still glowing, glorifying his own brilliance to Arthur. The two boys spent the evening just talking. They went to bed that night, each excited about the coming day. They woke the next day as if it was any other day. Really, they were both excited. They both attended classes that day, and Gabriel had no problem keeping up with the material. In fact, he excelled in his classes.

After that, the weeks just seemed to fly by for the boys. The weeks turned into a few months. The year ended with Gabriel integrating perfectly into the new curriculum. Then the summer came for the boys, and they returned to the Highland residence for the duration of that summer. They did much of the same things they had done the previous year, riding and exploring.

The time of the summer came when grades were in. As usual, Arthur's grades were good, but Gabriel still trumped his receiving all A's, even in his advanced classes. He was a brilliant child in so many ways, but just imagine if he'd never left the outer parts. Would he be in a vocational school somewhere in the country? He would be learning to do farm work or working on cars, learning little, not using his full potential?

The summer went by, Gabriel once again wrote a letter to his mother, but still no answer. So, he went on as he always had. As fast as the summer had gone by for the children they found as they went back to school, the time flew by very quickly. In fact, that year and the next few years just flew by, the boys doing much of the same day in and day out, riding and just being boys. Time went by, and the boys became older and bigger, now young men, pubescent and full of life.

Those younger years of youth had passed by like a brief flash of lightning, and they began their high school years, both still excelling at the school. Gabriel was, of course, young for his age, but he and Arthur were still thick as thieves. However, a new element had been introduced: girls. The school believed in having well-rounded boys, young men, really. So, they arranged socials with the Metropolitan Girls School three times a year. Gabriel always seemed a little awkward at those affairs, mainly because he had a strange sense of the female persuasion. After all, his mother and sister were estranged. Mrs. Highland was a shadow of a figure in the Highland family, and he'd been around nothing but boys and men for years. He found himself lost in that area of life.

His freshman year, they had three socials, a fall, winter, and spring event. At all three, Gabriel wanted to ask girls to dance, or at least just talk to them. Instead, he always sat at a table and played with the napkin or whatever would distract him and keep his mind off his own obscurity. On the other hand, Arthur was always the life of the party, dancing and sneaking kisses on the sly from the young women. He was often getting in trouble with the female chaperones of the Metropolitan Girls School. The men dare not scold him because he was a Highland. His father was always told of his indiscretions, but laughed and said, "How do you think I met his mother?" The board was less than pleased with Haw, but Mr. Highland carried a big stick around that place; They let the boy's antics slide. The year ended as any had, a summer at the Highland house, and grades to mark the midpoint.

A new year was to start, their sophomore year. It eventually came around, and the two boys were growing immensely. Their advanced studies were preparing them for their coming college years. The first semester went by, much like the first year of upper-classmen, socials, and such. The boys prepared themselves for the next year after another great holiday at the Highlands. Arthur celebrated his fifteenth birthday later that year and received his learners driving permit after a short test at the metropolis motor vehicles exam office. Mr. Highland bought Arthur a sports car so he could practice with his father around the city. Gabriel usually rode along now getting a better idea of the exact layout of the city. He often saw the same places he had seen for years, only now it didn't take hours to get there.

The Highland Boys School did not allow the students to have cars on campus. The boys would have to be picked up by the family driver and taken to the midtown district to learn with Mr. Highland. They practiced all the time after school, and Arthur became quite good. A few times, Mr. Highland let Gabriel drive. He thought it was fun, but Gabriel preferred his bicycle. The year did end, the summer passed, and the boys approached their junior year. However, Gabriel turned fifteen towards the end of the summer. Mr. Highland asked him if he wanted to get his driver's learning permit? Gabriel chose to ride his bicycle everywhere. He would occasionally ride with Mr. Highland, and Arthur when times arose.

The following year began for the boys, and eventually, like clockwork, the fall social came as the school year progressed, Arthur begged Gabriel to dance with at least one girl that night. It just so happened that both Gabriel and Arthur and turned into good-looking young men, and the women started approaching them. Gabriel was finally approached by one such girl and got the nerve to say yes to her advance and to dance for the first time. Halfway through their dance the next song began too fast for Gabriel, he panicked, left the floor, and only got in half a dance. Arthur still congratulated him on at least trying to get out there.

Gabriel found himself reaching inward for guidance about a lot of things. He had Mr. Highland and Arthur, but sometimes he felt alone. He didn't really understand why he was so shy when it came to women He was sure that he would come out of his shell, eventually. Towards the end of that year, Arthur got his license, and the boys often snuck off to ride in Arthur's sports car. The funny thing was that they had to ride their bikes an hour to get to Arthur's car. Now Mr. Highland made them ride their bicycles instead of picking them up. He knew that Gabriel liked the two-wheel ride better than the four, and he thought that Arthur could use the exercise as well.

Gabriel and Arthur both excelled that year. Gabriel had been writing in this creative writing class. He began keeping a journal of all that occurred in his life. Gabriel came to understand that year that he wanted to be a writer for sure. He felt if he had more time to do so, at that moment, especially on paper, he could express himself more eloquently. The end of the year finally came, and the boys took their AAT's (academic aptitude test) to determine which of the metropolis universities they would attend. They took their exams and went about the rest of the year. The summer was coming, and it would deliver their scores from the test to them at home.

Arthur did a lot of driving that summer going on dates with some of the girls he had met at the socials. Gabriel spent most of his time timing his journey's around the city. He knew every landmark and every street. He kept his journal every night. The boy's test scores came to the Highland residence towards the end of the summer around Gabriel's birthday. The perfect score for the exam was sixteen hundred. The test was scored in two parts: English and Mathematics. Gabriel scored perfect on his English, and seven-sixty on Math, a near-perfect score. Arthur's marks were almost the same, his combined score a fifteen-hundred and twenty, scoring equal marks on the two parts of the exam. Mr. Highland was indeed proud of the two boys. Their scores would get them into almost any metropolis they wanted. Now, all they had to do was make up their minds.

The summer pressed on, and eventually, Gabriel turned sixteen. Mr. Highland threw him a private party consisting of the whole family, just as he had done for Arthur the year before. At the party, Mr. Highland approached Gabriel. "Son, don't you want to go and at least get your driver's permit?"

Gabriel replied, "I don't really want to get it. Besides, I don't have a car."

"You know we could remedy that, but I thought you might say that, so I have something for you. I think the holiday keeper may have brought it early," said Mr. Highland.

Mr. Highland went to the back of the penthouse and retrieved a large item wrapped in paper and ballooned with happy sweet sixteen. Gabriel looked at it and thought it had to be a bicycle. It couldn't be anything else. Nevertheless, he went with excitement to open the gift. What he found he couldn't believe. It was a Paulo Gavali touring bike. It had to have cost thousands, he thought. It was a light silver metallic with blue and white decals, the finest gearing system, and a custom seat. It was just his size. He mounted the bicycle and began riding around the penthouse. He remembered how it felt that first time he rode a bike some ten years before, and it was beautiful. He said, "Excuse me, but I've got to go now."

He hurriedly made it to the door and met Clarence in the elevator. Clarence looked at him and said, "Is that a Gavali, Mr. Gabriel."

Gabriel was surprised because Clarence had never said a word to him in ten years. He said, "Why Clarence, it is a Gavali. Bottom floor, please."

Clarence armed the controls and set his sights on the first floor. When they got there, Gabriel was so excited that he almost fell getting out of the elevator. The front desk gave him a tip of the hat, and he was through the revolving door, once again. He didn't even wait for Arthur this time, he just went riding. He road for an hour or so, making his way to the heart of the city. He looked at all scenery, marveling at all of the buildings. He suddenly, remembered he had left his own party and headed back to the penthouse. Everyone was gathered and still laughing when he entered.

"We didn't think you were coming back," said Mr. Highland laughing and patting Gabriel on the back.

"Thank you, Haw," said Gabriel. "You don't understand what this means to me. It's the perfect gift. I couldn't ask for more."

"Once again, I think you're going to have to thank the holiday keeper on this one," said Mr. Highland.

"Whomever I need to thank, thank you. I'll write a story about the greatest gift I ever received, and this will be the subject, Haw," said Gabriel.

Arthur rejoiced with him and said, "You could've waited for me, man."

"Sorry, Arthur, there was no time," said Gabriel. "You can ride next time, maybe tomorrow."

"Tomorrow it is then, Gabe," said Arthur patting him on the back and motioning him back inside.

The family finished out the evening with a sense of joy and happiness. Gabriel was glowing and ever thankful for his gift. He spent the few remaining days of the summer with Arthur just being young men. They traded off nights, one-night riding, and the other night Arthur driving them around. It was an exciting time for the boys. They would be entering their senior year: Arthur seventeen and Gabriel sixteen. The two had worked hard, placed well on their entrance exams, and prided themselves in becoming well-rounded young men. Senior year at the Highland Boys School was always the best year. Having worked so hard, the school gave the boys a little freedom to relax and enjoy their last remaining time at the school. Their class load was smaller, and they were given a study hall to do whatever they pleased. Arthur was mainly excited to get through the first half of the year. He wanted to figure out where he wanted to go to school. Gabriel was excited for the same reason, but he had a feeling the two boys would go their separate ways. Gabriel knew he wanted to stay in the metropolis. He was in, but in their evening talks, Arthur had often spoken of wanting to go off to the far seas metropolis, mainly because he wanted to experience the foreign women. Gabriel was more concerned with getting a good education, more so than finding a mate, but if that happened, so be it.

Gabriel would be young for entering a university. I guess that was always what contributed to his shyness. His prowess in relation to women was also a factor in his shy nature.

The summer eventually ended, and the first day of school came around. There was always a buzz about the first day of your senior year. The teachers always made the students write an essay about their time at the Highland Boys School. If they were lucky, some even got published in the yearbook. Gabriel took this task very seriously, for he wanted so to have his writing published, just the first of many he hoped in the future. When the first period started, he knew just what to write for he had thought of the subject many times. It was always the same subject year after year. In fact, every ten years, the school published the most favored and inspiring essays, of which he hoped to get in as well. He only had two hours, but he made the best of it. It was plenty of time to execute a perfect essay. Gabriel had chosen a bold way of approaching the essay. He would write about his time there, leave out the names of those around him, but tell his story in full. He would write it, edit it and sign it anonymously in two hours. Though he knew by the mere mention of the camaraderie of his best friend's likeness, they would all know it was him, and they would be shocked. So, he did just that. He wrote with unbridled and unparalleled passion, not leaving out a detail of his life there, barely finishing in time.

Gabriel did not tell Arthur of his work of anonymity. He merely told him he thought he might have done well. The boys attended classes that day but snuck off the last period since it was their free period. They rode home through the city and into midtown, up to the penthouse, and began talking,

"Gabe," Arthur asked? "Have you made up your mind about school yet, I mean, where you want to go?"

"Nope, I've got half a year to decide," said Gabriel.

"Well, I guess what I'm saying is, don't you want to go to the far seas metropolis school with me? I'm pretty sure that's where I'm going. My father went there for two years."

"Well, yes and no, Artie. I kind of want to stay here, you know I love this city," said Gabriel sitting in the nook in the kitchen.

"But what about the foreign women? I hear they're wild, and besides, all you've ever seen is the country and this metropolis. Don't you want to branch out some?"

"Artie, I don't know how you got so far thinking like this. Maybe I want to see places just not now. I'm so young. And besides, I can't guarantee that I'll get into the far seas metropolis university. Unlike you, I really have to study and prepare for my classes. You, you just kind of show up, and it all works out for you. Besides, my father is not an alumnus," said Gabriel.

"Yeah, but you're smarter than me Gabe, and you have the scores to prove it."

"Thirty points!" Gabriel said, "That's what, maybe five or six questions and a missed proof on the whole exam? The reason I did better is that I studied for the exam. You're the smarter one, Artie. You just took the test and did that well, a near-perfect score. It took me, two prep classes to do as well as I did."

"Yeah, well, I didn't skip a grade. So Gabe, what do you have to say about that?"

"Well, I'm no good with women. I'd rather be good with women than having skipped a grade," said Gabriel.

"How can you say that? We wouldn't be where we are today. We wouldn't have the choice of even possibly going to the same school. Besides, girls are easy."

"Artie, there are a few months to talk about this. Let's just get some food and ride back home," he said placing his plate in the sink.

"Fine, but you're coming abroad with me kiddo, you just wait."

They walked into the kitchen and found Angela. She fixed them a quick meal, and they were off back to the dorms. They made a leisurely ride about it, for they really didn't want to go to sleep. Gabriel was thinking to himself about schools and Arthur all the way home. They arrived around ten o'clock and made an early night of it anyway. They knew the last year at the Highland Boys School was relaxed, but the grades still counted towards their university entrance.

They woke the next day and went to class, as usual, skipping out on the last period of the day. This time they rode straight to the penthouse and grabbed Arthur's car. They drove to the uptown district and to that famed bicycle shop so many years ago. Gabriel wanted some grip tape for his road bike, so they spent a few minutes perusing the selection and left. They went to that same old hotdog stand they had been visiting all those years, often being where they shouldn't be when they shouldn't be there. Although Gabriel was thinking of attending the local university, he asked Arthur,

"If I decided to stay here, we'd still meet in the middle, right?"

"Gabe, you've taught me a lot over the years. Mostly, how to be a best friend and a gentleman. We made a pact and a promise years ago, and I intend to keep that promise and pact. Puberty may have changed parts of us, but not the core, my friend. I still want to live and dream in this place you and I have visited so many times. I may want to wander, but I'll always call this place home. So, does that answer your question?"

"Yeah, I just want to know if I decide to stay, you'll still be my best friend," asked Gabriel getting into the little red sports car?

"Of course, Gabe. The family will take care of you just like always. They always have."

Gabriel thought to himself, what if I don't want them to take care of me? In his heart, Gabriel knew he had to break from the cradle that Mr. Highland had made for him. He needed to make his own way in the world, even though he was appreciative of the help all those years. Gabriel was sixteen, but he thought like a grown man. He dreamed of being that writer someday. Books, magazines, and newspapers, all of them appealed to him. He knew he needed to be free of distraction to hone his skills ultimately. He loved Arthur like a brother and the rest of the Highland family. But just as he was left alone on that doorstep so many years ago, he thought so shall I leave. They rode through the city, just listening to music for a while. They drove around the beltway driving at great speeds, Arthur weaving in and out of cars like a race car driver. In his heart,

Arthur still craved the fast life. He loved Gabriel just as much as Gabriel loved him, but he was a different breed from Gabriel. Gabriel somehow could not fill the gap he sometimes felt in his heart, the loss of his real family, his disdain for his father. At times he would find himself looking at Arthur and Mr. Highland, and knowing there was something there he had missed all those years. But still, he pressed on.

The boys made it back to the penthouse that night just an hour before they should probably be back at the dorms. So, they saddled their bicycles and headed home. They made it in record time, and it just so happened it was just about time for all the prostitutes and hoodlums to come out. They crept into their dorm, and they slept well that night. They woke once again to the buzzer at eight o'clock, made it to class, and started their day.

The first half of the day went by quickly, and the boys were off to lunch. They ate well and continued to the last few periods before their free period. But today the boys had some things to do during their free time. The main reason the school gave the boys the period was to give them time to start the process of their admissions to the universities. They reached the end of the day and went to the library. In the Highland Boys School library was a system that cataloged all the university entrance requirements and all the forms necessary for each submission. The boys had shirked their responsibilities thus far, but they knew they had to start sometime.

"Where should we start first," asked Arthur shuffling around some papers?

"Well, you're so bent on us applying to the far seas metropolis university, so let's start there," said Gabriel.

The boys went to the catalogs thumbed through until they found the far seas metropolis university (fsmu) and printed the necessary paperwork. The boys read the requirements to themselves, and suddenly Arthur cried,

"An essay! Heaven's Gabe, you know I hate essays."

"Artie, this is one of the best schools in the world, of course they want an essay. I'm sure all the schools you and I will apply to will require essays," he said laughing at Arthur's anxiety.

"Well, that's crap! I have an idea! You're better at this stuff than I am, why don't you write my essay," said Arthur.

"No offense Artie, but if you can't write an essay good enough to get into the far seas metropolis, how do you think you're going to do with the school work if you do get in?" asked Gabriel?

"I'll pay you, how's that?"

"No, Artie, now start thinking about what you want to say. We only have until six when the library closes. Think about how well-rounded you should be and then write," said Gabriel.

"Should be? What's that supposed to mean?"

"All I'm saying is sometimes on these things you have to tell them what they want to hear. They want to know what it is that's special about you, and what you will bring to their school. I just meant for you to remember all that crap they've taught us here, and remember they told us all that stuff for a reason. They knew it would help us get into these places. And besides, the school wants to look good in these things, you know make us look like perfect well-rounded gentlemen."

"So, what you're saying is to fluff this thing up," stated Arthur.

"Well, yeah. You need to tell them why you're good for them. You already know they're good for you, at least you think you know they're good for you."

"I'll bet mine is better than yours when we're done, what do you want to bet," said Arthur pointing his pen at Gabriel.

"I'll bet if you're trying to make this a contest, you're not doing the right thing. What exactly is the essay on?"

"Explain the greatest hardship you've ever experienced, had to overcome, and what you learned from it. Sounds like crap to me."

"You're going to have a hard time with this one. When have you ever had a hardship," asked Gabriel?

"I've had plenty of hardships!"

"Not getting the sports car you wanted is not a hardship," said Gabriel laughing.

"Oh, I suppose your life has been one big hardship. So, you left your family and got adopted by the second richest family in the metropolis, poor Gabe!"

"First of all, Arthur! I didn't leave my family, they left me here. And besides, you'll never know what it's like to not know your family; that's a hardship."

"Well, if it wasn't for my father, you wouldn't know the concept of a father."

"Haw is not my real father. My real father abandoned me when I was seven when he decided not to pay for my school. I am eternally grateful to you and Haw for all you've done for me, but yes, my life has been a bit of a hardship."

"Well, you can't write about your life in the country. Do you think the far seas metropolis school is going to let a country boy attend? I mean, they'll pity you, but they won't admit you."

"Oh, so you think people should pity me. Now we hear the truth. Do you think your father pity's me? What about Angela, Bethany, and James, do you pity them too?"

"They work for us. My father took them in and gave them a good life, a life they wanted."

"So, you're telling me, Artie, that the three people that work for your father, in his house, all want to work for him? I was adopted by him and given everything that they probably always craved. They're probably thinking, why didn't I live a life like Gabriel? Why wasn't I chosen to go to the school? And besides, they do have to hide where they were born. Pretty much everyone in the hotel hides who they are, just like me. If the word got out that your father employed so many people from the outer parts, do you think all these snotty little rich people would still want to go there?"

"You're one of those snotty little rich kids, Gabe, and don't forget that. That's how Angela and Bethany and James see you."

"I doubt that! You've never even been to the country. How do you know it's bad, maybe it's beautiful?"

"I don't think so, Gabe. Everyone knows the country is ugly. Everyone knows the metropolis is better, even the people from the country, remember that's why you're here."

"Have you learned anything from your father? All these years you've been saying that we're going to meet in the middle, you were still probably planning to run your father's empire, weren't you?"

"Look, Gabe, I've always had money, and I always will; there's no changing that. My father wants me to be well-rounded and humble. I mean you're my best friend, don't you think that makes me pretty humble?"

Gabriel looked at Arthur in disgust and grabbed his paperwork, left the room. He left Arthur to fend for himself on the essay. He retired to a small reading room away from Arthur and began his essay. In a similar fashion to his class essay, Gabriel wrote of youth and the loss of his parents. Gabriel did, however, write that his chance even to be writing the essay would not have been possible were it not for the philanthropy of one man. That man he left unnamed because he was so kind. He finished the essay just as the librarian was closing the place down. He didn't know what happened to Arthur. He tucked his forms and his essay away in his satchel bag and decided he needed a ride to clear his head. It was still light outside, but barely, but he went anyway. He left the seedy downtown area and headed for the midtown district. He rode at a furious pace until he reached the hotel and stared at the top floor from the ground. Maybe Haw meant well, he thought, but why was Arthur rearing his ugly inner feelings? Gabriel really had come to the thought in his mind that Arthur looked at him as an equal. Perhaps he thought the middle they had made their pact on, actually existed. He was sad to find out that this pact was not what turned out to be Arthur's true wish.

Gabriel headed out towards the city on his bicycle. He wondered, does Haw really feel as Arthur does? Does he pity me, or does he love me truly as his own son? Gabriel resided to something while on his way to stare at those buildings. He would live the rest of the year with Arthur. He would apply to two schools and two schools only. He knew he would get accepted to both that he applied to, but he also knew which one he would attend. He also knew he had to get Arthur into the far seas metropolis school. He knew he had the grades, but his essay wouldn't be good enough. So, Gabriel headed to the nearest coffee shop and began writing an essay for Arthur. He wrote furiously for an hour about how he had lost his best friend to a car accident when he was sixteen. He had learned the value of his life and the value of others' lives. He learned to grieve and to triumph in the end after a long period of time.

He finished the essay in about an hour, but then had to figure out how to switch Arthur's for his. He decided he would graciously apologize to Arthur and tell him what he wanted to hear, just like he told him to do in the essays. He started to leave the heart of the city, but stopped and made the resolution to stay close to his own heart and one day work there. He made the long ride back to the boy's school and arrived around twelve. Arthur was already asleep. He headed to sleep shortly after he got home, and slept feeling uneasy once again in his life.

The buzzer woke the boys at eight o'clock sharp. Arthur dragged himself from the bed and over to the window.

"Gabe," he said. "You worried me last night. I called my father to see if you'd maybe gone there. He said Bartleby had seen you out in front on your bicycle. Why did you go there?"

"I just needed some air, Artie," said Gabriel. "Let's just forget last night ever happened. I am grateful for you and your father, believe me, I am. I don't know what I was thinking about last night."

"I forgive you, Gabe. Just remember, we've sacrificed a lot for you. I haven't forgotten about the middle, either Gabe. I just want to wander for a while."

"Thank you, Arthur, now let's go to class then our free period and work on our essays and entrance papers," said Gabriel grabbing his things for the shower.

"Alright, Gabe."

The boys showered and readied themselves once again for another day in class. The day went by fast for the two of them, and the free period began. Gabriel had a mission now. He let Arthur write his essay and then placed everything in the envelope. Gabriel asked him to go check the front desk to make sure that's all they needed. While he was gone, he switched the essays. Arthur would never know.

They dropped the envelope in the mail along with Gabriel's submission, and the two went out for a ride to the penthouse. They arrived just in time for a surprise dinner with Arthur's parents. Mr. Highland briefly asked Gabriel why he was by himself in front of the hotel the day before. He gave Arthur a look and told him he must have been a few minutes ahead of Arthur. Bartleby must have gone inside while Arthur passed. Arthur went along with his story. He knew that his father would not like the story Gabriel would tell if he told the truth. They ate dinner in peace and comfort, and eventually, the boys left for home. They spent the remaining days of the week filling out more applications and essays and finished out the week having accomplished a lot.

On a rare occasion, Gabriel decided to stay on the campus for the weekend. He felt he needed some time alone. Mr. Highland called on Saturday afternoon and requested his presence, but Gabriel declined, saying he thought he might be coming down with a cold; he didn't want to spread any germs. Mr. Highland told him he was missed and that if he wished to, Angela could fix him some soup, and Arthur would bring it back. Gabriel thanked Mr. Highland and told him that wouldn't be necessary. He would be able to get some food at the cafeteria.

The weekend went by for both Gabriel and Arthur. Gabriel had some needed rest alone. Monday came and the buzzer sounded at eight, and the boys continued their time in class and used it wisely, as they always did. They left each day to ride, still alternating time on the bicycle and time in the car. Gabriel was aware that things had changed for the two of them. Arthur was oblivious to Gabriel's unhappiness and plan for change. The weeks flew by the weather now getting colder, and the boys attended the first of the three socials that year. Arthur was himself, dashing and brilliant while Gabriel once again sat in the corner.

The night passed slowly for Gabriel until a shy young woman caught his eye towards the end of the night. She was not necessarily the most attractive woman at the dance, nor the best dressed, but Gabriel felt compelled to talk to her. He walked over, not really knowing what to say. He mustered his frail ego and said,

"A girl so pretty should never look so lonely. My name is Gabriel, what's yours?"

The girl looked up and said, "I'm sorry I don't mean to look lonely. I've just had a bad week."

"Would you like to talk about it," asked Gabriel?

"It's kind of personal, and you're a perfect stranger, I don't mean to be rude," said the girl.

"Really, I have a good ear. What's your name?"

"Sydney, Sydney Bloomfield," said the girl.

"Okay, Sydney, Sydney Bloomfield, what seems to be the problem," asked Gabriel?

"I feel really weird talking to a complete stranger about this, but I kind of feel like you might be a good listener. Anyway, Gabriel, my mother, has fallen ill, and I can't take time off school to go see her."

"Is it serious," asked Gabriel?

"She has breast cancer."

"Oh, my that is ill. Why can't you go see her?"

"Well, I'm on an academic scholarship, and she lives far away. I can't take the time away from my classes because I can't lose my scholarship."

"I understand completely. I am also on a scholarship. What year are you?"

"I'm a senior. I'm applying to schools still, so I have to keep my grades up."

"Well, can you at least call her?"

"I've talked to her, but it's just not the same. Do you understand," asked the girl?

Gabriel sat down next to her and placed his hand on her hand and said, "I do understand the feeling of loss and not being able to talk to your parents. I think you're just going to have to take the time no matter what. Cancer is serious, and besides, your grades right now don't affect your acceptance that much. In fact, they won't see them until the end of the year after you've already been accepted."

"So, you're saying I should go then," said Sydney.

"It's your mother; you should definitely go."

A chaperone came over and said, "Gentlemen do not place their hands on young ladies' hands unless they are dancing, please."

Gabriel removed his hand, and the chaperone said, "Perhaps miss Bloomfield, you should make your way to the punch bowl and get yourself something to drink, alone."

Sydney gave Gabriel a look of thanks and got up from the chair and walked off. Gabriel lamented for a moment that he did not get to talk to her longer, but was proud of himself for engaging a young woman. The night went along with the two exchanging glances, but never talking again. The night ended. Arthur came over at the end and once again congratulated him on at least trying.

The two left the social and took a walk around the campus, Arthur begging questions of Gabriel. "We should hear about the schools soon, don't you think?"

"From what I hear, you usually have the news by the new year," said Gabriel.

"That's far off," said Arthur. "Gabe, I can't wait to get that acceptance letter, my grades are near perfect, and I know I did well on the essay too. There's no doubt that I'll get into the other schools, but I really want far seas metropolis university. Do you understand Gabe, wanting to be accepted to the greatest school there is? Well, it is, in my opinion."

"Artie, I'm sure we'll both get into the school, then we can travel the seaside together. It will happen," said Gabriel.

"I'm glad you feel that way, I've felt you were a little distant these last few months after that little tiff we had. You're not still sore about what I said, you know I'm humble, don't you Gabe? You know you're my best friend, right?"

"I know Artie, it's okay to disagree now and then," said Gabriel.

"Yeah, you know we never fight. I think the last fight we had until then was at the bicycle shop, do you remember that Gabe? That's the day you fell in love with cycling."

Gabriel laughed and thought to himself for a moment and said, "You're right Artie, we've never fought a lot, but sometimes I think we might take each other for granted. Do you agree?"

"I would never take you for granted, Gabe. You don't really feel that way, do you?"

"No, no, I guess I really don't feel that way. Maybe we should head back," said Gabriel.

"If that's what you want to do, Gabe. You're the man of the night, chatting up some poor lost girl. Come on, we have a long weekend ahead of us and a surprise in store for you," said Arthur.

The two boys headed back to the dorms and made it to bed by the one o'clock hour. Gabriel thought as he tried to sleep that the time couldn't fly by fast enough. He wished just to get the acceptance day over with, but that wasn't until February. He finally fell asleep that night and dreamed of a normal night's dreams and was awakened by the buzzer at nine. Arthur slowly came around and said, "Today, we see the mountains."

Gabriel, still half asleep, turned to Arthur and said, "What are you talking about, see the mountains?"

Arthur got out of bed and went over to the window looking out over the oak and maple trees and said, "Well, Gabe, I thought a lot about what you said some time ago. You said I'd never even seen the outer parts, well I have no want to see the country, but the mountains, that's a different story. I thought we'd go camping!"

Gabriel's initial thought was how odd. He asked, "Okay, so why now the revelation and how are we going to get there anyway?"

"I had James find us a map of the mountain country. He told me of a place he'd been when he was younger with his father. We've never really taken my car past the beltway," said Arthur.

"Is Haw going," asked Gabriel?

"No, Gabe, and he can't know. He can't know, you hear me."

"Fine Artie, but why do you want to go today," asked Gabriel?

"I don't know I just thought it might be fun. You know, see the woods and just because I've never been. Remember, I want to travel, but I don't know what it means to travel. Perhaps just a day of travel would help me get the fever. You know, since I'm going to be traveling abroad so much."

"I don't know about this. The mountains aren't the place for two young men. Perhaps we should rethink this, Artie."

"Nope, my mind is made up. Come on. Dress warm, my friend," said Arthur.

The two boys dressed quickly and got on their bicycles and started towards midtown. James had purchased some supplies for the two boys and packed them in Arthur's car. He had also gassed the car for the boys. They arrived around eleven and got into the car and headed east to the mountains. They passed the beltway, and Arthur tooted the horn and made a gesture with his hands waving goodbye. They rode for one hour talking all the way, both not knowing what to expect in the hours ahead. They followed the map that James had given them, and after another quarter of an hour, they reached their destination. They got out of the car and headed toward the entrance to the trail.

"Smell the air Gabe, it's fresh, and the trees. What kind of trees are these?"

"The air reminds me of when I was a child in the outer parts: it's clean. I'm not sure, but I think these trees are pines and some firs. You know, like the great holiday trees we've had in the past."

"Let's walk," said Arthur.

They grabbed their gear and started down the path looking at the birds, just taking in the beauty that the mountains hold. The pathway they followed was worn next to a small stream, and Arthur bent down next to the water and washed his face. He stood up and dried his face on his shirt and said, "The mountains are breathtaking, aren't they?"

Gabriel said, "We probably shouldn't go too far down the pathway. It's going to get dark soon."

"No, no, Gabe we're staying the night, my pack has a tent and all the supplies we'll need," said Arthur jubilantly.

"We're going to need a fire, Artie. It's going to get cold out here. Maybe we should set up camp now and walk later."

"Good idea Gabe, let's find a good spot."

They walked for about fifteen minutes until they found a pristine spot next to the water. There seemed to be plenty of wood and a lot of space. The boys undid their packs and set up camp. It took them a few minutes to get their camp set. They remembered some of what they had learned in their survival class in fourth-year physical education, but mostly they were improvising.

They finally finished camp and headed out on the trail. They explored for about an hour until they thought it best to retire back to camp. It would soon be getting dark. When they got back, they began collecting wood for the fire. They remembered small pieces to start and then big pieces to burn whole. They grabbed the kindling and made a small teepee out of the sticks placing leaves under the small hearth. They tried a few times but couldn't get the fire started. It was getting dark fast, so Gabriel began to worry. They tried a few more times and eventually got some smoke coming up. They blew into the kindling igniting the leaves and sticks. They placed large pieces on top, and soon they had a raging fire. It was just in time, for the sun had already passed beyond the horizon.

"What do we do now, Artie," asked Gabriel?

"I have a surprise for entertainment, Sir Gabe," said Arthur.

He reached into his bag and pulled out a bottle of whiskey. Gabriel said, "You've got to be kidding me, right. You think I'm drinking that you're crazy."

"Ah, come on, Gabe. We're out in the woods no one's around, what'll it hurt?"

"I've never had a drink in my life. You know that Artie."

"Well, now's a perfect time to have one. What do you say, Gabe? We'll toast to being best friends, and we'll laugh all night long. What could happen," asked Arthur?

"We could get drunk, get lost in the woods... I could name a hundred reasons not to," said Gabriel.

"Gabe, you've lived a chaste life, you've never kissed a girl. You're sixteen for goodness sake. Just take a drink and see what happens!"

"Fine! I'll make a deal. You let me drive your car home, at least some of the way, and I'll take a drink."

"Gabe, if that's what it takes, then fine, you can drive my car. If you wreck it, so help your soul."

"Alright, give me a swig then."

Arthur had only had a few drinks in his life, but he knew what whiskey tasted like, but Gabriel had no idea. He turned up the bottle and took a large gulp and spewed the alcohol out of his mouth, crying, "It burns, heavenly father it burns."

"It feels warm in your stomach, doesn't it," said Arthur.

"Fuck Artie, it burns," cried Gabriel grabbing his throat and salivating for a moment or two.

"Take another sip, the second doesn't burn as much as the first, I promise," said Arthur.

Gabriel reluctantly turned up the bottle again, and this time it went down and stayed down. Arthur took a few drinks, and they took a seat around the fire. It only took a few minutes for the alcohol to take effect. Gabriel said, "It's cold, but I feel warm."

His mind began to wander a little. He started thinking about school and his life with Arthur, wondering about his appearance. He became a beggar of questions of truth that alcohol can make us be. "Artie," he said, "Do you think I'm attractive? I mean, why don't the girls like me?"

"Gabe, if you knew how many women have asked about you around those socials, you'd be surprised. Your problem lies not in your looks, you're a dashing young man, but your problem lies in the fact that you're so caught up with the fact that you lost your mother and sister. You use it as a crutch."

"Oh, I do, huh. Well, let me tell you about your problem." The alcohol was raging through his system, feeling the angst of the past few months coming to ahead. "Your problem is that you're arrogant. I'm going to travel the far seas metropolis and play with all the horny little foreign women," he said, mocking him. "I'm so good looking, and I'm a Highland. I'll bet that if you get accepted, you'll fail out in a year."

"Oh, really Gabe, I'm arrogant? I'd rather be arrogant than sheepish like you. Come on, man, do you really think I think that much of myself?"

"I don't know Artie, when we were children, we made a pact."

"Oh, the pact," Arthur said, throwing up his hands. "Gabe, I've explained this to you a hundred times. I told you I'd honor that pact, just give me some time to be a man. Why do you want to live like we did when we were children? Is it because it was simpler? Is it because you're afraid to be a man?"

"I'm not afraid to be a man. I've been taught to be a man by your father and the school, but I just come from such humble beginnings, sometimes I can't get over that."

"Then, that's not my problem. My family has given you everything you could ever want. My father didn't have to take you in, but he did."

"There you go again, throwing that in my face. It's never equality. It's always repayment of services rendered. Here country boy! Here are some money and clothes, a penthouse, and a role model. Oh yeah, and don't forget the instant best friend, but you will always have those good deeds held over your head."

"Well, what if you had taken me in? Wouldn't you feel the same way, kind of like I owed you something?"

"No, because I didn't ask to be put here, don't you see that. I never asked for any of this. I don't know what it's like to have a father. I look at you and Haw, and I get angry, angry at my father," Gabriel said, slightly slurring his speech now. "Give me that damn bottle. OH! Did I mention that I feel lost? You've never been lost a day in your life, Artie."

Gabriel took another swig from the bottle and laid down in the leaves. Arthur thought for a moment and said, "Remember Gabe when I told you that first day you were at school how I wanted to go to an uptown school? Well as a child I told you I had a hard time dealing with the fact that I was in the second richest family in the metropolis. It's a different kind of loss, but it is a loss. Give me the bottle, Gabe. But unlike you, I learned to embrace the fact that it is better to have more than less. Look, we'll both get into fsmu, and we'll learn together."

Artie, how do you think I'm going to pay for that? It's one of the most expensive schools in the world."

"Gabe, you know my father will pay for it. He said he'd always take care of you, and he meant it. I promise you: he will."

"But what if I don't want him to pay for me, that's a big part of being a man, breaking away from the nest. Mine is a false nest. However, it is one I am thankful for. Don't get me wrong

Artie, I'm thankful. I just need to break away and learn to be a man."

"If you want to pay for school, I'm sure you'll get some financial help. If you chose to do that, but I don't understand why you would choose to do that, all expenses could be paid to the greatest school known to the collegiate world," said Arthur slinging the bottle around as he spoke.

"Let's just change the subject, Artie. I think these drinks are going to our heads, we're getting angry," said Gabriel getting up out of the leaves.

"Gabe, I'm not remotely angry, I'm just concerned for my best friend, my only friend."

"You're my only friend too, Artie. I'm sorry if I called you arrogant."

Gabriel got up from the ground and said, "Man, this stuff makes you have to pee." He stumbled off into the woods with his flashlight and began climbing a small hill to get away from camp. He urinated for what seemed to be an eternity, zipped his pants, and returned to camp. Arthur had started dinner and said, "Come and eat, my old friend."

They simmered a couple of cans of beans over the fire and boiled water for some instant rice. Over the next little while, they talked innocently. Gabriel felt bad about calling Arthur arrogant, the guilt and tears of the alcohol were taking over. They finished most of the bottle after dinner, and both decided it was time to sleep around ten-thirty that night. The embers of the fire were burning out, and the boys huddled into the tent, snuggling into their sleeping bags. They each told one another goodnight and that they were glad to be friends. Arthur, drunk, told him he was glad he was his best friend. Gabriel merely replied, I'm also glad we're friends, but he did not say best friends. Gabriel really had no other true friends.

During the night, they each got up to use the bathroom. Blind, in the dark, they both stumbled clumsily. Gabriel remembered hearing the noise of nearby animals and the sounds of the night, sounds he had not heard in years. Gabriel woke up early that morning with a raging headache. He was up just as the sun was rising and began cleaning up camp. He quietly cursed Arthur for the way he felt but cleaned anyway. Arthur soon woke and started helping him pick up camp.

"We'd best get going, Artie. We need to make it back before too long," said Gabriel.

Arthur agreed, and they finished packing up the camp and started down the trail. They followed that cold stream trail all the way to its head and put their things in the car. "You said I could drive Artie, remember."

"I guess I did, but if you wreck my car, I'll kill you," said Arthur.

Gabriel strapped himself in the car, backed out of the spot, and they were off. The roads were still foggy, but Gabriel navigated them well. They traveled for about forty minutes when Arthur told him he'd better take over. Gabriel requested he let him give the car gas on the next straight away, then he would give up the wheel. Arthur reluctantly said that was fine. In a few minutes, the two boys came to a long straightaway. As he wished to do, Gabriel gave the car some gas. Their speed climbed slowly, but they eventually reached one hundred miles an hour.

Gabriel began slowing down but did not realize he had passed a patrolman who had clocked them at ninety miles per hour. The officer sped up and positioned himself behind the boys. Gabriel immediately took notice. The officer turned on his lights, and the two boys began to panic. Gabriel, with his stomach in his throat, pulled the car over. Gabriel did not have his license if you'll recall. He began trying to make up a story, "Just fake your ankle is hurt Artie, trust me."

The officer approached the car and asked for registration and license. Arthur gave the officer his license and the car's registration. "Aren't you boys a little far away from home," said the officer.

"We're just coming from an overnight trip, sir," said Arthur.

The officer looked in the window and took notice that the boys had given him Arthur's license. "I'm going to need to see your driver's license, please," said the officer to Gabriel.

Gabriel being an honest man, said, "I don't have a license, sir."

"Will you two boys step out of the car and move away from the vehicle please," said the officer.

Gabriel and Arthur stepped out of the car. They moved around to the backside of the car and were told to sit down in front of the patrol car. "What are we going to do now, Artie," asked Gabriel?

"Just be quiet Gabe, everything will be fine. He'll just probably let us go," said Arthur.

The officer began searching the car with a fine-tooth comb, opening the glove box, and then eventually searching their camping bags. The two boys thought they had nothing to worry about until Gabe said, "Shit! I put the rest of the alcohol in my bag." Arthur just sighed.

In a few minutes, the officer emerged with the bottle of alcohol, as Gabriel knew he would. He said, "Boys, you're in a load of trouble. Could you stand up and put your hands behind your backs, please."

The officer cuffed the boys and put them in the back of the patrol car. Gabriel began blaming Arthur for bringing the alcohol. Arthur began blaming Gabriel for wanting to drive, even though he didn't have his license. The officer called for a tow truck for the boy's car, and then made a U-turn in the road and headed for the patrol station. The boys were quiet now, Arthur knew he'd have to call his father. Gabriel wondered what would happen to him since he was speeding and had no license?

They arrived at the patrol station, and the officer led the boys into the station. He sat them down on a bench and asked whose parents they were going to call. Arthur spoke up and gave the name and number of his father to the officer. The officer then took off the cuffs from the boy's wrists. The officer dialed the number Arthur had given him, and James answered the phone,

"Hello, Highland residence."

"This is officer Cuthbert of the Chesapeak patrol in the mountains of the east parts. I need to speak to Mister or Misses Highland, please."

James didn't exactly know what was going on, but he knew it couldn't be good.

"I'll get Mr. Highland for you, officer," said James, and he went to find Mr. Highland. In a moment, James found Mr. Highland in the study and told him there was an officer on the phone. His immediate reaction was panic, what had happened to Gabriel and his son? He rushed to the phone and answered,

"This is Ignatious Highland,"

"Mr. Highland, I've got two young men here in my station in possession of alcohol and driving pretty fast without a license. One of these boys says he's your son," asked the officer?

"Yep, they're mine, where are you," asked Mr. Highland in an exhausted tone?

"Chesapeak in the east mountain parts, sir," said the officer.

"The outer parts! What the hell are they doing out there?"

"I'm not sure, sir, but you're going to have to come and get them, they're in some serious trouble," said the officer.

"I'll be there within the hour," said Mr. Highland.

He hung up the phone and told James to call the car and get ready. He needed some help finding this place. He went into the study and to the safe and grabbed a large sum of cash. The elevator came and took them to the lobby. They went out of the revolving door to the car that was waiting outside.

"Where to Mr. Highland? Oh, hello, James," said the driver.

"Chesapeak, in the east mountains," said Mr. Highland.

The driver headed out of the cobblestone drive and towards the eastern highway. They reached the highway in under five minutes and were headed towards Chesapeak. Mr. Highland was surprisingly calm considering the situation, James hoping the boys didn't let on to his involvement. They passed the beltway and on towards the mountains making good time.

"This is Arthurs doing James. Gabriel wouldn't do such a thing. All these years of letting him run free have finally caught up with me. Where did he get the alcohol," asked Mr. Highland?

"He is only six months from drinking legally, maybe he has an ID," begged James.

"Legal or not, why were they out there."

"I don't know," said James.

Mr. Highland and James were quiet the rest of the way. Mr. Highland was upset that he was being put in this sort of situation. He would make Arthur learn a lesson. They drove for another forty minutes and arrived at the patrol station. Mr. Highland told James to stay in the car, and he went into the station. He found the two boys scared and worried about what Mr. Highland would do.

"You must be Mr. Highland," said the officer, "These boys are in a lot of trouble, sir. I don't know if there's too much you can do for them."

Mr. Highland placed an envelope on the counter and said, "I believe you'll find that the boy without the license, his paperwork is in here. As for the alcohol, I believe I left it in the car last time we went camping. I know these boys very well officer, they wouldn't cause any trouble at all."

"His paperwork may be in that envelope, but this took up a lot of my time. I could have been catching other criminals. Our time as patrolmen is very precious, you know," said the officer.

"I'm an avid supporter of the patrolmen in my area," said Mr. Highland, "Perhaps I could make a donation to your office? I donate a thousand dollars every year to our officers, how's that sound?"

"Two thousand and I'll even give you passes to the outer parts officer's gala," said the officer.

"Then we have a deal," said Mr. Highland.

"Have a nice day, Mr. Highland, and keep them boys out of trouble, ya hear."

Mr. Highland motioned to the boys to go outside, "Arthur, James will drive your car. Boys in the limousine, please."

The boys hanging their heads in shame hurried towards the car. The three of them got into the back of the car and drove away, James followed closely behind in Arthur's car.

"Father, I'm sorry," said Arthur, "We were just having a good time. Please don't be angry."

"Arthur, I don't want to hear it. All the trust I give you, and you repay me this way. I just spent two thousand dollars in under two minutes. Gabriel, I know you're not innocent, but I'm pretty sure Arthur put you up to this," said Mr. Highland calmly fuming.

"Haw, I'm sorry it was all my idea, please don't be mad," said Gabriel.

"Father!" said Arthur.

"I don't want to hear it," said Mr. Highland. "Since you have no respect for my time or my money, here's what's going to happen. Both you and Gabriel are going to work off that two thousand dollars starting next weekend. You both will work the door with Bartleby until the year is over. And by the way... the car is mine. Arthur, it's about time you learn some responsibility. Gabriel, you should know better. I expect better of you."

"I'm sorry to disappoint you, Haw," said Gabriel.

The boys hung their heads and became quiet. The rest of the car ride home was silent, the boys realizing exactly what they'd done. They made it home that afternoon. They got on their bicycles and rode back to the school, dreading the week ahead of them. Now instead of looking forward to acceptance day and their letters, they had commoner's labor to deal with.

The boys didn't speak to each other for the rest of the week. They went about their schoolwork and attended class. The weekend came, and the buzzer went off at seven-fifteen, they had to be at the hotel by nine. They made it out of bed, not saying a word to each other, readied themselves, and made it to the hotel by five of nine; Bartleby was waiting. He showed them the ropes of being humble, then left them to do their jobs parking cars.

The boys continued working after school and on weekends for the next few months, Mr. Highland not even allowing them to go to the winter social. The fall semester came to an end. Gabriel and Arthur talked at times about their letters, but most of the time, they were busy working. The season of the grand holiday was near, and the two boys worked diligently. Arthur pleaded to his father to let them stop working, but Arthur had been becoming increasingly humble, having to work as a layperson would. Gabriel was satisfied with honest work and was glad that he was repaying Haw for all he had done for him. The holiday season began, and the boys had easily paid off their debt. Mr. Highland thought the boys were progressing well, so he made them keep working. Arthur resented his father. He told Gabriel several times that a man of his background should not have to work, Gabriel just laughed at him. Eventually, Mr. Highland let the boys keep their money. Arthur was so full of himself that he gave it to Gabriel, saying only the people of the outer parts worked like this, he shouldn't have to. He didn't need the money; he was a Highland.

The gap between Gabriel and Arthur was widening. It was apparent to Mr. Highland, but he thought, at last, my son is learning something. All those years of freedom had taught him to spend and be frivolous. But even in his punishment, he did not learn. It seems Arthur had only begun his disdain for his father. Arthur would confide in Gabriel often about how he felt his father was unfair. Gabriel took great pride in remembering that this was honest work for people like him. Nevertheless, the two boys trekked on. Mr. Highland gave them a break the week before and after the great holiday because he felt they deserved it.

It was letter time, and the new year was approaching. The boys watched the mail carefully. It was three days until school started and much to Gabriel's surprise his letters began to arrive. He chose to wait to open them until Arthur's arrived. It wasn't until two days later that the bulk of his letters arrived. Two letters of great importance arrived from the far seas metropolis university. When James brought the letters in, Gabriel smiled, but Arthur was nervous. Arthur applied to four schools only in case he didn't make it into the far seas. The family gathered for dinner that night; James, Angela, and Bethany were present.

"Open yours first," said Gabriel.

Arthur acquiesced and began opening his letters, saving the far seas for last. One, two, three acceptances, and the sweat on his palms began to show. He stopped and said, "Gabriel, I only have one left, the most important one, now you open yours, and we'll open the far seas letter together."

Gabriel agreed, but he only had two letters. Letters one he opened and was accepted. Then he waited for Arthur. "Now together," said Arthur.

They both opened their letters at the same time and read carefully. The two paused for a moment. Arthur looked as though he was teeming with excitement, and Gabriel was poised for whatever news he may get from Arthur.

"I got accepted," said Arthur jubilantly. Mr. and Mrs. Highland gave him a well-deserved hug. The work his father had been making him do seemed not to matter at that moment. Arthur was ecstatic. He paused for a moment and looked at Gabriel,

"Let's have it, Gabe, come on."

Gabriel paused for a moment and said, "Looks like we're still going to be roomies!"

Both Mr. Highland and Arthur ran to give Gabriel a hug, for he deserved it. The moment was festive for all, Gabriel safe in his secret of changing the essay. He knew it was because of him that Arthur got in. They celebrated through the night, Gabriel content in the fact they both had been accepted, triumphant in his secrecy.

School started back for the boys and work as well. The month of January was cold. The boys abhorred work, but acceptance day was just around the corner. The weeks and weekends flew by. Bartleby was proud of his young apprentices. Eventually, the first week of February came, and the acceptance day was at hand. There was a graduating class of forty, and all had decided on where they would continue their education. The ceremony was long. Each student had his places of application and acceptance read, and then they gave their choice for admission. One after one was read until Arthur's turn arose. "Arthur Highland," came from the speaker's voice. They read off his schools, including the Far Seas Metropolis University, and there wasn't a student or teacher unappreciative of his achievements.

"What school do you choose, Mr. Highland," asked the speaker?

"I choose far seas metropolis university, Mr. Speaker," said Arthur.

The crowd clapped for him. He was well-liked, but had only one close friend. He looked to Gabriel and gave a nod as if to say you too, my friend. Arthur had finally had his moment and he was proud just as every Highland man before him had been. The ceremony continued and after about nine names, Gabriel's came up. The speaker told of his two applications, his two acceptances, especially the one pertaining to the far seas. The speaker said,

"What school do you choose, Mr. Liden."

Arthur was waiting for his answer, knowing they would be going to the same school and would remain best friends for the remainder of their lives.

"Mr. Liden, your answer?"

Gabriel cleared his throat and with a proud smile, said, "The Metropolis University." Arthur thought he had heard him incorrectly and he went to the speaker and said,

"He meant the far sea metropolis university, Mr. Speaker."

Gabriel stood proud and said once again, "The Metropolis University."

Arthur rushed to his side and said, "What are you doing man, are you crazy, Gabe?"

"No, Arthur, I'm going to where I want to go, not where you want to go," said Gabriel.

Arthur was in disbelief. He couldn't believe his ears. Why would his best friend do this to him? Gabriel turned and sat down and listened to the remaining eight student's achievements. Arthur just sat in silence. They left the ceremony just after it ended and went their separate ways. Gabriel went to work, and Arthur to his dorm.

Gabriel arrived to work and began greeting guests, Bartleby was right by his side. Around seven, Mr. Highland's car drove up, and Gabriel opened his door. Mr. Highland stepped out and asked,

"How did the ceremony go?"

"As expected, Haw," said Gabriel.

"You chose our Metropolis University didn't you, Gabriel," asked Mr. Highland?

"Yeah, how did you know?"

"Gabriel I've raised you from the time you were a young boy. You're a worker, you don't care necessarily about the most prestigious school in the world. The difference between you and Arthur is that Arthur needs a school like that to get him, well, anywhere. He thinks he's owed everything. But if he can prove himself at a school like that, he can be his own man. You're already your own man, and you're only sixteen years old. You take responsibility for your actions, Gabriel. Only you showed up to work today. That says a lot about you, and even more about Arthur."

"Thanks, Haw, that means a lot to me coming from such a successful man," said Gabriel.

"Go on, take the night off," said Mr. Highland. "Oh, and by the way, It would be my privilege to pay for your school. Just keep that in mind."

"You know I can't accept that Haw... but thank you."

"I thought you might say that. Then let's leave it at this, if you need a co-signer come knock on my door, son," said Mr. Highland. "Have a good night, Gabriel."

Enjoy Your Night Gabe...

Chapter 6

The Gavali

After the talk with Mr. Highland, Gabriel took his Gavali out for a ride around town. He still didn't know what to say to Arthur. He had made the best decision for himself and the ones around him. He knew that Arthur would think he was ungrateful, but he had made his decision. As he often did, he made it to the heart of the city and just marveled at the buildings, once again dreaming of working in that very district. Gabriel toured the city until he grew tired and knew he had to face Arthur. He started back to the school, eventually reaching the seedy downtown district. He snuck in through the gate and walked his bicycle up the cobblestone driveway and to the dorm. He walked up the stairs to that same door he had stepped through so many years ago and opened the door. He found Arthur sitting at his desk turned towards the window and just watching the world go by, and he said,

"You said to me years after we made that pact that we'd meet in the middle, but you have no intention of keeping that promise. You deceived me, and you used me and my family," said Arthur quietly brooding, turning away from the window.

"Artie, do you even know me? I didn't deceive you. I told you I didn't know if I wanted to go to the far seas or not. And remember, I never asked for all of this, but my feelings for you and your family are genuine," said Gabriel. "It's just time to break away. Don't you see why I did it, Artie? You need to become your own man too. We all think so."

"Who's we," asked Arthur in a raised tone of voice and standing from his chair?

"The whole of your family, Artie," said Gabriel clenching his right hand into a fist and then pointing at Arthur. "You once said you'd had money and you will always have money, but that doesn't make you a man, it just makes you spoiled."

"You're jealous, aren't you?"

"What jealous that your father respects me more than he respects you? Why would I be jealous of that," asked Gabriel?

"My father loves me more than he could ever love you, just remember that Gabriel Liden."

"Herein lies the question. Would you rather be loved or respected, Artie? I'll choose respect."

"Don't call me Artie. Well, I guess if you think about it, you're right, you have gained people's respect, but no one ever has loved you, have they, Gabriel?"

Arthur got up from the seat and started gathering his things, placing them in a suitcase.

"Where are you going, ARTHUR," asked Gabriel stroking back his hair in frustration?

"I've arranged for you and me to have separate rooms for the remainder of the year, so I'll be leaving after tonight for the far side of the dorm."

"Don't you think that's a little childish, Arthur," said Gabriel.

Arthur didn't say a word. He just kept gathering his things and placing them in his suitcase. After a few minutes, Gabriel left the room and went to the gymnasium. He entered the building and thought of his inception and orientation so many years ago. He lamented because Arthur had been such a good friend. He hated for it to end this way. He decided to go and stay at Mr. Highland's for the night and let Arthur cool off.

He went to his bicycle and rode all the way to midtown and into the Metropolitan Plaza. He rode up the elevator, but a new person was there, someone he didn't recognize. He left the elevator lost and exhausted and he knocked on the Highland's door at one a.m. and James answered.

"I take it things didn't go well with Arthur," he said. "Please come in."

Angela came to the door dressed in her robe and said, "Poor boy, let me fix you some tea. Come on."

They went into the kitchen where Angela put on some water for tea. James and Angela both sat and listened while Gabriel told them what had happened. He told of Arthur's disdain for him, and that he had claimed the family didn't really love him. Angela chimed in and stopped Gabriel from talking,

"Gabriel, you wouldn't dare believe what Arthur has said. We all love you, especially Mr. Highland. Arthur is just angry right now."

"Yeah, but what do I do about it? I have to live with this family for six more months," said Gabriel. "What about summer?"

The tea kettle whistled. Angela went to the stove and pulled it off the eye. She reached for a cup in the cabinet and poured the water into the cup. She placed a tea bag in the water and returned to the nook, listening as James explained his point of view.

"Gabriel, I've seen you go from a boy scared and uneducated to one of the brightest young men I've ever met. Arthur feels threatened by you. Before you came, it was the Arthur show, and he was the only star. Then you came, and we all shared our attention. Arthur was fine until he realized that we loved you as much as we loved him. He always wanted to be first. You're a more well-rounded person than Arthur, and he knows it. That's why he feels disdain for you. Don't let it bother you."

"He's asked for a separate room at school. He won't allow me to stay here this summer," said Gabriel attempting to sip his tea.

"If he gets his way, there are a few options. The summer is only a couple of months away. We can put you in a suite by yourself, or we can ask Bethany if she would let you stay with her. I'm sure she wouldn't mind," said James tapping his fingers on the table and leaning forward in his seat.

The tea was finally cool enough to drink. Angela said, "It's an herbal tea, it should put you right to sleep,"

Gabriel drank from the cup as the three kept discussing the predicament between himself and Arthur. James told Gabriel he would speak with Mr. Highland in the morning. For now, they should probably get to bed. After all, Gabriel still had to ride to school in the morning. The three adjourned for the night, Gabriel to the same room he had slept in so many times during breaks from school. He tried to sleep but was too worried about his future, not necessarily with Arthur, but the rest of the family. The hour of seven came very early.

He rode through traffic at seven-thirty, trying to get to school in time to shower and be ready for his first period. The traffic was heavy, but he made headway through the cars and busses and arrived around eight forty. He readied himself and was off to class.

The first period crawled by, and Arthur was a no show for class, Gabriel began to worry. By the second period, Arthur was in class but had switched seats to be as far from Gabriel as possible. The third period came, and the headmaster was waiting at the door for Gabriel.

"Gabriel, one of the board members wishes to see you. Please go to Mr. Riley's office." He left the class and walked across the campus to Mr. Riley's office, where he and Mr. Highland were sitting in the office having a pipe together.

"You wanted to see me, Haw," asked Gabriel?

"Yes, son, come on in," said Mr. Highland. "Gabriel, Arthur came to me with some accusations of stealing his things. We all know he's just acting out, so let's cut to the chase. I talked to James this morning, and he conveyed your concerns. I understand where you're at Gabriel. Arthur is my son, and I listen to his concerns as well. Now you two are going to be split up as are the wishes of Arthur, but I know you still are an equal part of my concerns. As James said, Arthur suggested you not stay at the house for the duration of the summer, so I'm going to arrange for you to have a suite, and Bethany will stay and look after you. She's always wanted to live at the hotel."

"That sounds like an amicable solution, but Haw I'd like to keep my job if possible through the rest of the year. I'd also like to request a spot with you while I'm in school next year if that won't be a problem," asked Gabriel standing and waving away the smoke from his face?

"That shouldn't be a problem, son," said Mr. Highland. "You've earned my respect over the last number of years, and if that's what you want to do, I will grant you that request. Just do me a favor and stay out of Arthur's way. There's no telling what kind of stories he's liable to come up with these days. Now go back to class, and we'll see you at the hotel around five." Mr. Highland turned away from Gabriel and engaged Mr. Riley in conversation and they continued their pipe smoking.

"Thank you, Haw," said Gabriel.

He left the office and endured the rest of his classes that day before he made his way back to the hotel to work his job. He continued this same routine until the end of the school year, eventually graduating from The Highland Boys School. There was no celebration on the day of his graduation. Instead, he had to move his things to a suite on the thirty-eighth floor, as Mr. Highland had instructed him to do.

He arrived at the hotel by way of limousine around five, and Bartleby met him at the car. He helped him to the elevator, and Clarence asked,

"Why the bags, Mr. Gabriel?"

"I finally graduated, but I'm staying on the thirty-eighth floor now. Miss Bethany will be staying with me."

"Thirty-eighth we go then, Mr. Gabriel," said Clarence.

He manned the controls, and they were off. It took only a few moments to get to the floor. Clarence lowered the gate, and Bethany was waiting for him. Gabriel went into a similar door as the Highland penthouse, went inside and moved to the back bedroom, and unpacked his things.

He took the weekend off at the request of Mr. Highland. He enjoyed several rides through town. Bethany watched over him when he was home, and every once and a while, James and Angela came down. Mr. Highland made a daily visit after the first few days, making sure he had enough money and food to eat. Mrs. Highland even came down to see him once. He had not seen her in months, for she usually retreated to the reading room and away from the family each night.

The summer moved along for Gabriel, and eventually, he had to find an apartment to live in during the school year. Mr. Highland offered to help him find a place that would suit him, so they went looking one day just before school began. They looked all day in the heart of the city in the loft district, and then towards the end of the day, they landed on a beautiful studio overlooking the skyline. Mr. Highland knew he would need a co-signer because of his age. But since Haw was Haw, he talked the leaser into letting him have it by himself. Mr. Highland gave the landlord two free nights at the plaza.

All was set for Gabriel. He had a steady job, financial aid, and a place to live. All that was left was time and work. The last few weeks of summer passed, and Gabriel took the last bit of his freedom to heart. He spent his seventeenth birthday alone with Bethany, enjoying a small gift she had purchased for him. He received a small gift from the Highlands with a rather cold card wishing him good luck that year. He rode that night through the city for hours then returned home to eat with Bethany before retiring to bed. Time moved by swiftly, and the day to start school eventually came around. Gabriel had moved in the night before only taking his clothes. He had no furniture or possessions other than his Gavali and camping gear. He figured he would buy furniture as time went by, but for now, he had to worry about studying and paying for his rent. Mr. Highland's reputation was on the line, and Gabriel took that very seriously.

He acclimated well to the University atmosphere, studying, writing still in his daily journal, and earning his keep honestly. The first semester went by, and he made excellent marks as always. He took the time of the great holiday to prepare for the coming year. He missed the time he would normally be spending with the Highland family, but he was an independent man now. He chose not to partake in the parties of the school, for he knew he was there to learn to be a writer, not a drinker and philanderer.

He made excellent marks in his second semester and the third, and so on. He went straight through the summers, always working at The Plaza and honoring his mentor Mr. Highland by paying his rent and bills on time. He was always so focused on school that he forgot to engage any women. He still felt awkward, and that had not changed at all.

His senior year came around, and he was on a pathway for a Magna Cum Lade graduation. He was now nineteen going into his last year. He studied diligently, and his efforts would pay off. The first semester ended, and he began applying for jobs. He applied to every magazine and newspaper in the city and started interviewing. The next semester ended, and he had only three classes to finish to achieve his original goal of being a writer. He was set to graduate just before he was twenty, just after his last summer semester. He knew he always had several offers lined up. There was one job in mind that interested him more than the others. He had applied to a magazine called the Metro Cyclist, which wrote mainly about tours and scenic routes that cyclists could use in the metropolis as well as other metropolises. He would be a research analyst for the magazine if he did well in the final interview.

It was only one week until graduation, and Gabriel dressed in his best attire and took the bus to the magazine's office. He walked in and sat down and waited for a few minutes. The receptionist called his name and told him to go into the last office on the right. He got up and brought his portfolio with him and a picture of his Gavali bicycle. He made his way to the office, and a rotund man sat in the room.

"I'm the editor of the Metro Cyclist, Miles Davies is the name," said the man in the office. "You must be Gabriel Liden?"

"Yes sir, glad to meet you, Mr. Davies," said Gabriel extending his hand and leaning forward.

"Call me Miles, Good lord son, how old are you? No offense, but you look like you're twelve," said Mr. Davies pulling his glasses halfway down his nose.

"I'll be twenty in a few weeks."

"What are you a genius? I see you graduated from University and you went to that boy's school before that. I don't like people smarter than me. It makes me feel weird around them like they're thinking greater thoughts than me. You don't think greater thoughts than me, do ya," asked Mr. Davies twirling a pen in his right hand like a drumstick?

"I'm a humble man, Mr. Davies. But if you must know why I'm so young and looking for a job, it is because I skipped a grade when I was younger and then went straight through the summers at the University, sir."

"Look me in the eye. Miles, call me Miles. I'm a University man myself Gabriel, graduated, well, twenty-five years ago, worked my way right up to a senior editor. So, son, let's cut to the chase. You made it through the first two interviews, so you gotta have something about ya. So why do you want to be a research analyst," asked Mr. Davies now tapping his pen on Gabriel's folder?

"I've been riding through this city for thirteen years, ever since I was a really young man. I know everything there is to know about this city, every restaurant, every park or venue. From what I understand, the job entails gathering and analyzing information about the city for the magazine. I can map out perfect routes and beautiful scenic routes safely through midtown, uptown, the heart of the city, and even downtown."

"Well I don't know about downtown, aren't you a little young to be going down there, son?"

"The Highland Boys School has been around for a long time when this metropolis was pretty young, and it is located in downtown. I rode through there all the time," said Gabriel.

"Okay, so maybe you know the city, but what do you ride around town, what kind of bicycle do you have? How true you are to the sport?"

"Here, I have a picture," said Gabriel.

"Well, let me take a look-see here."

Gabriel pulled the picture from the stack of papers he brought with him and showed it to Mr. Davies. He looked for a moment, put the picture close to him, and said with surprise, "Hey, that's a Gavali custom. Where'd you get that? Never mind, you went to the Boys School. Your parents are probably loaded."

"Actually, my parents are dead, have been for a long time."

"Shame to hear that, hope I didn't offend you, son."

"No, I came to grips with that a long time ago. So, what do ya say, Miles? Want to give me a shot?"

"Don't get ahead of yourself, kid. It's long hours and little pay. But I like you; You look honest. Answer me this; what are your long-term goals with the magazine?"

"I'd like to be a columnist and maybe an editor someday," said Gabriel proudly boasting his future quiet ambitions.

"Another pipe dreamer! Everyone wants to be a columnist. Alright, Gabriel Liden, it is Gabriel, right?"

"Yes, Miles."

"Alright, you graduate in a couple of weeks, and you'll probably need to give notice at your current job, says you work at The Plaza, right?"

"Right."

"Okay let's say three weeks from now I want to see you on this doorstep with computer and notepad in hand. Never mind about the computer, we'll give you one. Wait! We'll give you a notepad too. Just show up in three weeks, son. Have a good day."

"Thank you, Miles. You won't regret it!"

"Yeah, they all say that, son."

"See you in three weeks, Miles."

"Now run along," said Mr. Davies.

Gabriel was elated. He left the building, knowing he was on a path to becoming a great writer. He celebrated that night by calling into work and treating himself to a ride through uptown. He slept wonderfully that night and was off to finish the rest of his semester. He called Mr. Highland and told him the news. He told him he would be giving him his notice, but he was eternally grateful.

He finished out the semester and had one week of work left. He planned to take a couple of weeks' vacation before starting his job at the magazine. The weeks went by terribly fast, and Gabriel was off with the freedom to start his research. He rode for hours on end, mapping out routes and marking places day after day. As the third week ended, he finally took a day to rest.

The morning came early with the buzzer sounding at seven a.m., but he was up to the task. He dressed casually and rode through traffic; it was a hot morning. He arrived at work at a quarter until nine, strolled through the front door, and began his ascent to writing stardom. He met the receptionist with a smile that said he was glad to be there and he said,

"High, I'm Gabriel, remember me. Stella, right?"

"Good morning Gabriel, welcome to your first day, and here is your first assignment. You need to bike to the corner of Haight and one fifty-first to pick up our order," said Stella.

"Haight and one hundred and fifty-first, I know that wait, I know that address," said Gabriel.

"Of course, you do. It's the Happy Donut.".

You'll do well, Gabriel...

Chapter 7

Meet Again

Now you're probably asking yourself, didn't he promise me a love story, and you're right, I did. But the basics of Gabriel's life had to be told for you to understand how truly great his love story was, what he had to overcome.

Gabriel went through a number of months picking up the donuts, but eventually, he started actually doing some analysis for the company. Mr. Davies grew more impressed with him daily and he was promoted to copy editor after a long few months of work.

Time flew by for Gabriel during that time. He celebrated his twenty-first, twenty-second, and then his twenty-fourth birthday, where he was promoted to a columnist, the youngest in the whole of the magazine. He had little social life for the next few years, rarely dating and focusing on his work, perfecting his column for each month's issue. He occasionally rode to midtown and looked at the plaza where he had once lived. His relationship with Mr. Highland had dwindled to mere letters every six months. Arthur, well Arthur, was following in his father's footsteps, except for his philanthropy, of course.

Three more years flew by for Gabriel, and he was promoted to a senior columnist after a brilliant piece on safety and knowing the right way to ride through the metropolis. On his twenty-eighth birthday, Mr. Davies announced he was moving to another metropolis to begin his retirement. This placed openings in the magazine for top jobs, and Gabriel set his sights high.

A few weeks went by, and Mr. Davies was set to retire in two days. The announcement of who his replacement was going to be that very day. The morning went by slowly for all who were positions to be promoted. Mr. Davies called a meeting at twelve o'clock sharp, and all senior columnists and junior editors were to attend. Ten o'clock came and then eleven, and soon all were gathering in the conference room. The newest research analyst had brought donuts from the Happy Donut for the occasion, and all helped themselves to crullers and glazed donuts aplenty. Mr. Davies entered the room and sat at the head of the table,

"Now you're all wondering what's going to happen next. There are two spots that will be available, one junior editor will become senior editor, and one person will move into his or her position. Now all of you have been doing a fine job, a lot of you here for ten years or more. Whoever gets the promotion to senior editor will take over my position as of today, and I will help you get going before I leave. Whomever I decide to promote to the junior editor position will start immediately with the respective pay increase and extended vacation time allotment. Now you know I'm not one for making a scene of things. Everyone in this room is suited for these jobs, but Mr. Caraway, you have proven yourself above all and will assume my position as of today."

Gabriel was a little disappointed that he didn't get the senior editor position, but he still had a shot at a junior editor. He crossed his fingers and hoped his name would be called to fill the position.

"As for junior editor taking Mr. Caraway's position, there really was only one true choice. This person just celebrated his twenty-eighth birthday, Mr. Liden you're now in charge of all main stories and headlines."

Gabriel couldn't believe his ears, he stood up and gave great thanks to Mr. Davies and a hearty congratulations to Mr. Caraway, his new editor. In eight years, he had risen from the ranks of the lowest analyst to one of three junior editors now overseeing three senior and five junior columnists, and not to mention a new office with a window. He finished out the day beginning to learn some of the ropes from the other editors. He ducked out at four-thirty for a rare celebration with some office co-workers.

They all met at the One-Fifty-One pub in the heart of the city at five and began celebrating. All gave jealous congratulations to Mr. Caraway and Gabriel, who had a rare celebratory drink. If he ever drank, his choice of drink was whiskey from the southern metropolis, not far from where they all lived. He never had more than one, but today he accepted a second. It, after all, was a special occasion. The alcohol had given him special powers, powers of perception. He had noticed a young woman sitting at the bar, but as usual, he didn't feel he could muster the personality to charm her. Gabriel was still a virgin, but that doesn't mean he was ignorant. His co-workers convinced him to go and talk to her. She was not the prettiest girl in the bar, nor the best dressed, but he felt compelled to get to know her after the liquid courage had reached his veins.

The young lady looked as though she'd had a rough day, so Gabriel searched his mind for something witty to say. He walked up to her and said the one thing that had almost worked in his past,

"A girl so pretty should never look so lonely."

"That's funny. I haven't heard that line in ten years or so," said the woman barely turning around towards Gabriel.

"No, I mean it, you're very pretty, and you do look terribly lonely," said Gabriel cupping his hands and unnoticeably checking his breath, or so he thought.

"No," said the girl. "The reason it's so funny is that some guy from one of the boy's schools gave me that line about ten or eleven years ago, it was kind of a bad time for me," said the woman wrapping her left hand around her drink and tapping the glass with her right hand.

"May I ask what boy's school, because I went to one of the boy's schools," asked Gabriel now with his right hand behind his neck and leaning forward slightly?

"I'm pretty sure he went to The Highland Boys School, we always had socials with them," said the girl.

"I went to The Highland Boys School."

Then in his slightly inebriated mind, it dawned on him that maybe this was the girl he had given advice to so many years ago. Then he said,

"Your name isn't Silvia or Cynthia or something like that, is it? I gave that line to one other girl in my life, and that was at a social." Suddenly he seemed to sober rather quickly. He straightened up and stroked back his hair shyly with both hands.

"My name is Sydney. Actually, you were close. What else did you say to that girl," asked the woman?

"She was having some type of trouble, I think her mother had cancer or something," said Gabriel widening his eyes then closing them to think more accurately.

"You have a good memory, Gabriel, wasn't it," asked the girl?

"You remember my name?"

"Of course, actually, the reason I'm here today has something to do with you," said the woman.

"How do you mean," asked Gabriel?

"Do you know what today is, Gabriel," asked the woman? "No, well I'll tell you. Today is the ninth anniversary of my mother's death. She died of breast cancer at the ripe old age of fifty-two. So yes, Gabriel, my mother had cancer. But the reason it applies to you is that you told me to go and see her, and I did. I almost lost my scholarship, but I got to see her one more time, so thank you, Gabriel. Do you have a last name?"

"Liden, Gabriel Liden."

"Well, Gabriel Liden, it's nice to see you again. You were a great influence in my past, so let's see where the future goes; have a seat," said Sydney patting the seat next to her.

The two began talking to one another over the celebratory crowd of his co-workers, and time passed wonderfully fast. One by one, his friends left the bar and headed home, but Gabriel and Sydney talked until the eleven o'clock hour. He happened to glance over at one of the televisions and saw the Metropolitan Plaza on the screen. He asked the barkeep to turn it up,

"Today hotel mogul and board member of the Highland Boys School, Ignatious Hawthorne Highland, passed away due to heart complications at the Midtown Mercy Hospital. Mr. Highland is survived by his son, who will inherit his empire, and his wife of thirty years, Jean. The memorial will be held Sunday at the metropolis cemetery. And on to other news..."

Gabriel stopped for a moment, put down his drink, and Sydney said, "Did you know him, Gabriel?"

"Mr. Highland raised me from the time I was six years old. I just received a letter from him five months ago," said Gabriel. "Sydney I'm afraid I'm not feeling too well, I think I'm going to have to call it a night."

"If you feel you must, but is there anything I can do to help," asked Sydney?

"I'd like to do this again, will you give me your number, and I'll call you soon," asked Gabriel putting a fifty-dollar bill on the bar?

"Sure thing, Gabe."

"You called me Gabe. I haven't heard that for a long time. I'm sorry, I've got to go now."

Gabriel put her number in his phone, paid both of their tabs, and left out the front door. His bicycle was still at work, so he started walking home. He soon realized he had had a few too many drinks, so he hailed a cab passing by, got in, and rode home in silence. He thought to himself in his fogged clarity, I must go to the service, but Arthur will be there. Maybe after all these years, he will have forgotten about such childish things that had happened between us. He made it home around midnight and passed out with the beginnings of a raging hangover.

His alarm sounded early that morning. When he awoke, his head pounding, his body deprived of water and nutrients. He wanted to get an early start on the first day of his new job, so he took a cab and made it in at eight o'clock sharp. He made it to the coffee machine with his thoughts not on his new job, but on Mr. Highland; he prayed he did not suffer. The staff showed around nine, and he began to get more focused. One of the junior editors Sam was showing him the ropes that day,

"Did you hear about the guy from the Metropolitan Plaza, you went to the Highland Boys School right," asked Sam?

"Yeah I knew him well, he was like a father to me,"

"Sorry to hear that. Let me show you these proofs for the next issue's cover," said Sam.

He listened, but his heart was not necessarily in it. The day went by slowly for Gabriel, but when five o'clock rolled around, he left promptly. He rode his bicycle to the coffee shop where he saw the headlines on the paper. They called "Haw" the second richest man in metropolis and talked about all the good he had done in his too-short life. Gabriel drank his coffee and lamented for deep down he knew that Haw was the only father he had ever really known. Even though their contact was only through letters every six months or so, he would miss that interaction. He resigned himself to making a brief appearance at the memorial. He knew there was nothing else he could do, and Haw would not be happy to see him lose his new position because he was stricken with grief.

He rode home and decided that he would call Sydney Sunday night and ask her for some company after the services; he thought he might need some. He tried to work on his proofs Friday, but his thoughts kept meandering. He decided to go out for a walk around nine o'clock through the heart of the city. There was a baseball game that night and the streets were crowded. His mind kept coming back to his childhood with Haw and Arthur. Suddenly, he was waving at a passing bicyclist he had known for some years and was reminded that he had just met a wonderful young woman and received a promotion for a job he loved. His mind was put to some rest.

Saturday came and he spent most of the day working on his proofs for the new cover, often thinking of Sydney. His thoughts randomly touched on Haw and Arthur. How would Arthur be? The day seemed to get away from him, and the hour for bed neared at eleven o'clock. He needed to be wide-eyed and respectable for the funeral; the whole family would be there, not just Arthur.

He slept well that night and woke to the sunlight in his little studio in the heart of the city. The service was at noon, and he went for a small ride through the city before dressing himself for the services. He arrived at home at ten o'clock and showered and began getting dressed. He was ready by ten-forty-five, so he ate a small breakfast before he called the cab. He was a twenty-minute drive in traffic, so he called the cab for eleven-twenty-five.

The cab arrived a few minutes after eleven-thirty, and he was off down the elevator to meet the car. When he got in the cab, he settled in for a strange ride. The grief he wished so much not to have turned to sorrow, and he wept silently in the back of the cab. He cried for all the years Haw had loved him. He cried for all the years that he had acted as his father, even though he tried not to admit his own father had abandoned him. The car ride was long, but eventually, he reached the cemetery, and a large crowd had gathered. There was a small private service for the family in the church of the great giver. It was only an hour or so before the public ceremony.

Gabriel chose to stand in the back of the crowd and waited for the hearse to arrive. It arrived promptly at twelve o'clock, along with a motorcade of four cars. Angela, James, and Bethany were in one car while Mr. Highland's wife and Arthur were in another. The other two held Mr. Highland's mother, sister, and her daughter, while the other held the minister and his wife.

They stepped out of their cars, and the pallbearers did the deed of placing the casket on the gravesite. Mrs. Highland and Arthur, along with the rest of the family, made their way to the front row of the seats, Arthur keeping his mother and the other girls from crying. It was quite a spectacle, this funeral. People had come from all over the metropolis, and beyond, to attend the funeral. They paid their last respects to a philanthropist and a good friend. The service started just after twelve. When all of the family was settled, the minister began his prepared memorial.

"Do not mourn the loss of our friend Ignatious Hawthorne Highland,' said the minister, "For he rests in a wonderful place now, free of all pain and suffering; free from the ills of the world; he has transcended now."

Gabriel stood quietly in the back, listening to the eulogy, trying to keep his emotions under control. The minister spoke for a good half an hour and then relinquished the task of closing the service to Arthur. Arthur rose from the second seat next to the casket and up to the microphone. "My father was a great man. He taught me to be strong and kind, merciful, and ever thoughtful. He took care of his family and those he loved, never questioning if one of them asked for something. My father once told me the most important thing about having the burden of wealth was trying to give it back to those who needed it. In my father's honor, for the next few days, the hotel will be running a half-off special on all rooms. On this day of grave circumstances, may you all leave with the sense that Haw, as they called him, loved you all and is safe from all harm now, thank you."

The minister gave the okay for all to give their offerings, and the ceremony was through. Angela, James, and Bethany slipped off into a limousine while all placed their flowers and mementos on the casket. The custom of shaking hands with people began shortly after the body was lowered into the earth. Gabriel waited until the last person went up and made his way up to Mrs. Highland and Arthur,

"Hello, Arthur," said Gabriel.

"Gabriel." said Mrs. Highland, "How good to see you, my you've changed so much I almost didn't recognize you. How are you, son?"

"Yes, how are you, Gabriel, it's good to see you," said Arthur placing his hands behind his back and giving a slight nod to acknowledge him.

"I just wanted to pay my respects to Haw. He did a lot for me over the years," said Gabriel.

"You mean we did a lot for you over the years," said Arthur looking away briefly before catching Gabriel's eye.

"Yes, I guess that's what I meant. So, you're taking over the business, huh?"

"Yeah, I guess we both knew I always would. I just didn't think it would be this early, you know," said Arthur. "Let's take a walk. Mother, excuse us."

"It was wonderful to see you, Gabriel," said Mrs. Highland.

"And you as well, Mrs. Highland."

"I don't guess you keep up with school affairs too much, do you, Gabriel," said Arthur walking with his hands behind his back.

"No, not really, I mean your father just let me know things were going well in his letters,"

"Yes, the letters. We found all of them when we were cleaning out his study. I'm glad you two kept in touch. There was one letter that was not postmarked. I'm guessing it was meant to be sent to you in the future; I don't believe it was finished. I didn't read it, but whatever went on between you and my father was between you and my father. Our affairs have been separate for years. But about school affairs, you didn't get the ten-year publication of essays, did you?"

"No, I guess I kind of severed ties when I left," said Gabriel looking briefly at Arthur as they walked along the pathway.

"Well your senior essay was published, I'm guessing it was yours, it was anonymous, but we all knew it was you. It caused quite a stir among the alumni. Of course, you know my father was probably the reason it got published."

"Of course, I'm honored," said Gabriel.

"I'll send a copy over to you. I got your address off of one of the letters, so I'll have a courier send it to you. Well, Gabriel, Gabe, it's been a pleasure, but you'll understand I have a lot to take care of."

"I understand. Arthur, I just have a couple of questions, where are you living now, are you married?"

"I'm living on the thirty-eighth-floor suite, and no, I'm not married. We'll have lunch, but I've got to go, for now, Gabe. Until later. And by the way, good luck in whatever you're doing now. I'm sure you're doing well."

"Goodbye, Arthur."

"Goodbye, Gabriel."

Gabriel turned and walked away, his letter in his coat pocket. He knew he would never see Arthur again. He decided to walk home and take a leisurely stroll about town. After all, it was a beautiful September day. He had to finalize his feelings. He had to read the last letter and let things go. He walked to a nearby coffee house and got an espresso and sat on the patio. He pulled out the letter.

"Dear Gabriel,

I hope you're feeling okay. It has been a few months since we've written to each other. The business is going well, but I feel I'm getting old. I went for a checkup at the doctor the other day, they say nothing's wrong, but I'm tired all the time. By the way, I read your last article in the June issue, a brilliant piece on the scenic midtown. I especially enjoyed the part where you told all to stop into The Plaza for an exquisite brunch on Saturday or Sunday. I'm sure it'll help business, thanks. Mrs. Highland sends her wishes as well as Angela and the crew. They all ask about you all the time, and I tell them you're doing extremely well. I hope you're getting by, and I know you're still living in that old loft in the heart of the city. If you ever need any help you know you can ask, I'd be happy to help. I laugh because I've put that in every letter since you left here, and not once have you asked for help. You're a strong and independent man Gabriel. You know I've always admired that about you. I'm feeling tired now, but I'll write some more later. I've got the August issue, and I'm ready to read it. So, I'll pick this letter back up a little later."

Gabriel was happy that despite feeling tired, Haw was doing well before his heart complications. He got another espresso and just sat and thought about his life, how well his professional life was going, and really how privileged his childhood was. In his heart, he thanked Haw and Arthur as well, together the two had made him mostly who he was. Suddenly, he remembered he had meant to call Sydney, so he pulled out his phone and pulled up her number, and dialed.

The phone rang for a moment, and after five rings, he was sure he was going to get the machine, but she answered, "Hello, this is Sydney."

"Sydney, hi this is Gabriel Liden calling, how are you?"

"Well, considering you past the two-day rule, I'm surprised," said Sydney.

"I'm not sure what you mean," said Gabriel shuffling his phone to his other ear.

"Well, usually, when a guy tells you he's going to call you, he makes the call within two days, but here it is the third day, and you're just now calling."

"Sorry, I've been tied up with work and the funeral and everything, but I was calling to see if you'd like to get together tonight. I'd love to see you."

"Tonight, I don't know that's pretty short notice. Do you know what a girl has to go through to get ready for a date?"

"Well, not really, uh, no."

"Well, let me tell you. First, there's the dress, then the hair, oh, and don't forget the shoes and makeup, but if you..."

"Okay, I understand all that. Do you still want to go out?"

"Yes," said Sydney.

"Fine then. I'll swing by at seven," said Gabriel looking at his watch.

"I'll be waiting with bells on. Oh! By the way, I'm the second house on Virginia after Commons," said Sydney.

"I know the area well, see you at seven," said Gabriel.

Gabriel called a cab to come to pick him up, and it arrived in about twenty minutes. He got in and headed for the heart of the city, excited about seeing Sydney again. He arrived home at five o'clock and undressed, took a shower then tried frantically to find dinner reservations. As he was dressing, he thought, spicy, not spicy, upscale, or just average? He suddenly remembered a fondue restaurant in the uptown area, and that's where she lived; it was perfect. He called the restaurant, and they had a seven-thirty reservation available, so he booked it.

It was now six, and he looked and realized that his place was a mess, so he started shoving things in closets and under the bed. He had probably entertained two or three people in the entire time he had lived there. For the most part, he was a solitary creature. He straightened the artwork on the wall and did a once-over in the kitchen. He went to the curb to hail a cab.

"Virginia and Commons," he said, and the cab was off. There was another baseball game that night in town, so there was a little more traffic than usual, he began to worry if he'd make it on time. He desperately told the cab driver to hurry. He couldn't be late.

They turned on Virginia from Commons and pulled up to the second house, he told the driver to hold on, and he went to the door, it was exactly seven o'clock. He knocked on the door, and after a moment, Sydney came to the door.

"One minute late, I don't tolerate tardiness," said Sydney looking at the clock on the wall.

"Well, dear madam, if you would've answered the door in a timely fashion, I wouldn't have been late. By the way quickly, the place we're going is in uptown do you want to walk or take a cab, there's one waiting out front?" Gabriel turned and pointed at the cab and then turned back towards Sydney.

"So, I see. No. I can put some flats on. We'll walk," said Sydney briefly closing the door and going inside.

Gabriel turned and went to pay the cab driver. By the time he returned, Sydney was waiting on the front doorstep, flats on, and ready to walk. They started off down Virginia and Gabriel said, "If I remember right the restaurant is only three blocks from here, I hope you're hungry," said Gabriel as they walked.

"If I were a proper lady, I would tell you... I could eat, flutter my eyes, but I'm starving, so let's hurry, okay," said Sydney jokingly in a no-nonsense matter of tone.

They made a brisk walk of it talking the whole time, mainly just small talk, to begin with, trying to rehash the whole of the other night. Gabriel had a fogged memory of the night they met due to the alcohol, and he was embarrassed. He told her he probably has a drink once a year. She said that was okay because she was twice as bad. She drinks twice a year, once on the anniversary of her father's death, somewhere around February, and secondly the day of her mother's passing. He told her that as a young adult, he never felt the need to drink, even with the passing of his parents. She asked,

"When did your parents die?"

"When I was very young, actually," said Gabriel looking down as he answered.

"Then who raised you, your grandparents?"

"Actually, I didn't know my grandparents, and my parents I knew very little. Mr. Highland and their family raised me from the time I was six," said Gabriel.

"You said he was like a father to you, but I didn't know you meant literally. Where did you live?"

"I lived at the dorms during the year and at the penthouse suite on the top floor of the Metropolitan Plaza during the winters and summers all the way through high school. I broke most of my ties when I was sixteen, although I worked at his hotel through college," said Gabriel.

"Where did you go to school after The Boys School," she asked holding her clutch at her side?

"Metropolis University. My best friend Arthur at the time wanted me to go to the far seas university, but I didn't see a need in wasting all that money," he said.

"You got into the fsmu?"

"Yeah, but our Metropolis University was just as good for what I was trying to do."

"Interesting, Gabe. You had a unique childhood and later youth, but I am sorry your parents passed at such a young age, that must have been crippling," said Sydney looking towards Gabriel as they walked down the street together.

They continued walking and Sydney, focusing on his childhood, which made him a little uncomfortable, however. He kindly asked her, in lieu of today's events, that he'd rather not talk about the Highland family. She understood, and they talked a little bit about the weather and how nice it was for the time of year. They reached the restaurant at seven twenty-five and were seated by seven-thirty.

"I've never been here, what made you pick this place for a first date? Do you bring all the ladies here," asked Sydney in a dry tone?

"There have never been a lot of women; I'm actually quite shy. I've hit on probably four girls in my entire life, and with you, well you, I hit on you twice, so there you have it."

Sydney giggled and smiled as they brought out the pot and oil for the meats and vegetables. She liked his looks for he was a fit young man, although sheepishly shy, he was witty. She thought to herself, could he be this good of a man, to have been raised so lavishly and still turn out so humble. Gabriel grabbed some meat and put it in the pot to fry, and he began answering her original question,

"Back to the first question you asked a minute ago, why I chose this restaurant. I'd like to tell you I've been here a million times, but the truth of the matter is that I needed a good place fast. I kind of didn't think ahead for this little outing. I wanted to, but I spent the last few days swamped with work and thinking of long-lost friends."

"Do you spend a lot of time on your work? You work for a magazine, right?"

"The magazine's called the Metro Cyclist, and yeah, I kind of do spend a lot of time on work. But I also spend a lot of time riding my bicycle. I have a Gavali," boasted Gabriel as he stirred the oil.

"Is that a good bicycle? I don't know much about them," she asked.

"It's pretty much the best bicycle you can buy. It was a gift from Haw, I mean Mr. Highland."

"Haw, how cute," said Sydney grinning slightly.

"That's just what the people close to him called him. It comes from his middle name Hawthorne, so you see Haw. I called him that from a very young age. Hey, maybe we could go ride bicycles in the park this week, would you like that," asked Gabriel looking up from his plate?

"We'd have to go right after work, but that sounds good to me. You know it's getting dark earlier now," said Sydney.

Sydney seemed to hang on to his every word while Gabriel was surprised. She found him interesting, but he too was smitten. They gazed honestly at her during the conversation, both having wondering flashes of longevity and promise from very early on. They continued talking over dinner, each trusting what each other said, something elementally valuable to a great future loving relationship.

They finished dinner and decided to head just down the street to a small café for coffee and dessert. They talked as they walked, passing the quaint shops of uptown.

"We've talked a lot about what I do and my life, but you seemed to have left out exactly what you do most of the time Sydney," asked Gabriel.

"Wow, you must have been drunk the other night," said Sydney with a quick laugh and a look to the street.

"I'm sorry, have we already been over this? I'm sorry Sydney, I care and really want to know, so please just humor me again, please," said Gabriel turning a slightly rosy color.

Gabriel grabbed her hand as they walked down the street, and Sydney began to blush. They were an adorable match, just walking down the street and sharing secrets.

"I'm in real estate, mostly residential. I received a degree in psychology from the Midwestern Metropolis University and then stayed there and got a master's in the same field. I worked with the children's hospital for a while, but after spending so much time with sick children, I began to get disillusioned. My ex-boyfriend was in real estate. He got me a job in his firm. He did mostly commercial real estate though, and I learned the ropes of the metropolis homes and lofts. Where do you live, Gabriel?"

"I live in the loft district in the heart of the city. I've lived in the same loft for twelve years. I probably could have owned it by now, but the location is perfect for work and is central to all the districts of the city, what about you? How long have you been on Virginia," asked Gabriel?

"Oh, about two years. After my ex and I broke up three years ago for obvious reasons, I rented for a year and then bought this place," said Sydney.

"What do you mean, obvious reasons?"

"He didn't want to commit, but it's a little more complicated than that," said Sydney.

"How do you mean complicated?"

"He tried to push things in a certain area of the relationship and left others to die. When I told him how things were going to be, he decided to leave instead of stay."

"Show me where he is, I'll get 'em. You just show me. If he hurt you, I'll kill 'em, that's what I'll do," said Gabriel in a joking manner.

"You're so silly, Gabe. Okay, how come no one's snatched you up yet?"

"Hold that thought."

They arrived at the coffee house and requested a table for two on the patio. They were led to a small table by the street with a candle and a small glass dish full of cubed sugar.

"Ah, now that's better, we can rest our feet," said Gabriel as he stretched his legs.

When they had settled in, Gabriel reached across the table and grabbed her hand. "Now, what were you asking me before," he asked her politely?

"Why no one has got a ring around your finger," asked Sydney?

"It's not very complicated; I've just never put myself out there."

"Don't you get lonely, though?"

"When I was a child, even though I lived among a wonderful family, I learned early on how to be alone. I know how to entertain myself, but I'm not really sure how to entertain others all the time. Does that make any sense," asked Gabriel looking down at the coffee menu?

"I thought we weren't talking about your childhood, Gabe," said Sydney. "But I understand what you mean. I had to learn to live by myself. When you do that, you find that when you try to entertain others, you forget your manners or you speak of taboo subjects. Sometimes you just think it's all a hassle."

"Is tonight a hassle," asked Gabriel?

"No, tonight is wonderful Gabe, thank you."

They continued conversing for an hour or so, and the conversation never ceased. Sydney kept reaching down every once and a while, making contact with Gabriel's hand and arm, affirming the connection between the two of them. Every so often, they would laugh, and there would be a moment of silence, but good silence. That silence was filled with what if's and affirmations. Is he going to kiss me? Should I let him kiss me? What will he say next? What will she say next? I wish she would touch me. I enjoy it when she touches me. The thoughts were aplenty about the other at the table, not wandering and wishing to be elsewhere. It was getting late, and Sydney said,

"This is the best time I've had in years. But unfortunately, I have to show a house at nine a.m., so would it be rude to call it an evening, and make a promise for that bicycle riding adventure this week?"

"You have truly captivated my interest Sydney, thank you for a wonderful evening. Let me walk you home, and we'll plan on the middle to the end of the week. Sound good?"

"Sounds perfect," said Sydney.

They paid the tab and began walking down the street towards Sydney's house. They still talked and laughed all the way through the main street of Virginia, eventually reaching the doorstep of Sydney's house. They both paused,

"Well, I guess this is goodnight, Gabe," said Sydney.

"It's been truly wonderful, but I feel a little anxious. I would love to kiss you goodnight, but I feel that sort of an embrace could be satisfied by the anticipation until we meet again."

"You are truly a gentleman. That school of yours did you well, you know," said Sydney.

He stepped up to the stairs and reached down and gave her a warm hug and a kiss on the cheek. Once again, she blushed, and Gabriel stepped away and made sure she got into her home safely. He stood for a minute, taking in the moment. Sydney looked out the window, waved, and was off to sleep. She hoped to dream of him.

He walked down Virginia until he hailed a cab and was headed home. He made it to the heart of the city, but there was traffic from the game being let out, so he paid the cab driver and walked the rest of the way home. He made it home by midnight and was off to slumber dreaming of his beautiful new infatuation. Beautiful Dreams Gabriel...

Chapter 8

Together, Alone

Gabriel woke the following day feeling refreshed and excited about life. He went to work working on the final proofs and copy for the latest issue, but all he could think about was Sydney. Gabriel wanted to call her but resisted the urge and went on with the day. He was in such a good mood that he took a short ride during lunch and then finished the day. Traveling home, he went and thoroughly cleaned his home. He figured he would be entertaining her in the future, so he went to the store and bought some things for the house. He purchased some frames to frame his artwork because his place still looked the same as when he was in college. He bought some candles because he knew every woman loves candles. He also bought some groceries in case she would be hungry if he brought her back. All of these things made the night go by pretty quickly, and then he made his way to bed. Once again, he dreamed of Sydney and what their second meeting might entail.

He woke invigorated the next day, and again, saw the day fly by with anticipation. He got home, and not unlike a seventh-grade boy, looked at the phone a few times, wanting to call her. They said the middle to the end of the week, and that was tomorrow, so he picked up the phone and called her number. The phone rang a few times, then a few times more. Then the machine answered. Her message played and the beep sounded,

"Hi Sydney it's Gabriel, I mean Gabe, um well, we had talked about getting together to ride in the park tomorrow, so um, if you want you can call me back and we can um, set up a time for tomorrow if that's good for you. Alright, just waiting to hear back, you've got my number. Bye"

Gabriel hung up the phone and began the wait we have all endured, the agony between, and if the suitor calls back. He knew that she would call back, but it was just a matter of occupying the time until then. He walked around the apartment, singing to himself and listening to music. He started with classical, and then to rock, and then finally to the blues. He was overflowing with excitement and failure at the same time. Perhaps she did not have as good of a time as she led on. He continued to listen to the blues in his home when at eight-after-nine, his phone rang. He ran to the other side of the small studio and answered the phone,

"This is Gabriel!"

"Goodness, Gabe you scared me, were you expecting someone important?"

"Yes, I mean no, the phone just scared me; I was knapping," said Gabriel slowly pacing.

"Uh-huh, you were waiting on me to call you back, weren't you, that's cute," said Sydney in a playful voice.

"Yes, I was waiting for you to call me back, but I dozed off."

"Is that why the music is so loud in the background, Gabe?"

"Fine, Sydney," said Gabriel in a calm voice, "I was waiting for you to call me back, and now that you have, I'm happy."

"Me too, Gabe, and by the way, I would love to go riding tomorrow. I'm showing a house in that part of town, so I'll be there around five. How's that sound?"

"It sounds wonderful. I can't wait to see you," he said with a sigh of relief.

"Gabe, there's only one problem, well two in reality. One I don't have a bicycle and two, a very important two, I haven't ridden a bicycle since I was twelve. There was a brief silence on the phone."

"Well, Sydney, there's that old saying, it's just like riding a bike. You never forget, and besides, you can rent them at one of the old shops I go to."

"If you say so, Gabe. I have to run now. I'm sorry, I have a lot of paperwork to finish before the morning. I have a closing at ten," said Sydney.

"No, I completely understand. Tomorrow at, well, let's say five-fifteen?"

"Very well. See you then," said Sydney just before she hung up the line.

Gabriel hung up the phone, and his mind was at ease. He cooked a late-night meal, read some in a novel he was reading, and then headed off to bed. He slept well in anticipation of the next day and dreamt of beautiful things.

He woke at the normal time and arrived at work at nine sharp; he had things to do that day. He was clearing the final proof for the cover of the October issue that particular workday. His new job was tedious, but he also got to write an editorial every month. This month's column was on the famed Gavali. His piece told of when he first received his gift and the many tours he had given since receiving the bicycle. It was his first piece as an editor, so he wanted it to be brilliant. He spared no story or account and would finish it before the week's end. But five o'clock was closing in, and he was excited as usual to go for a ride and, especially to see Sydney. He left around four-forty-five just to make sure he got there on time.

The park was busy when he got there. He wondered would he be able to commandeer a bicycle for Sydney. He hoped one of his friends was working in the shop that day. Five fifteen rolled around, and Gabriel was sitting at the bench in the center of the park. Five twenty turned and still no Sydney. He began to wonder, would she show? Perhaps something happened to her, he thought. But out of the corner of his eye, he saw her approaching hurriedly. Gabriel pretended to start walking off, and she moved faster,

"Gabe, Gabe, I'm here."

Gabriel kept moving, laughing as he walked faster and farther away.

"Gabriel Liden, wait, wait," said Sydney loudly through the crowd.

He suddenly stopped and turned with a smile and said as she approached, looking disheveled,

"I thought you didn't tolerate tardiness," Gabriel said in a joking manner.

Sydney laughed as she caught her breath.

"You did that on purpose, didn't you," asked Sydney pulling back her hair and wiping her brow?

"What, walk away, you betcha," laughed Gabriel holding on to his prized Gavali.

"You made me chase you, is that how our relationship is going to be, me chasing you, huh," Sydney said laughing and still trying to catch her breath.

"I have a feeling no one is going to be chasing anyone in this relationship," said Gabriel with a coy grin on his face.

"So, you are saying you wouldn't chase me if you had to," said Sydney smiling, putting her hair back into place and running her hands down her shirt to straighten it.

"I've chased a lot of things in my life, and if you happen to be the next thing in line, then so be it, but I prefer an amicable relationship, don't you?" said Gabriel holding on to his bicycle.

"Amicable," said Sydney. "What about passionate and frivolous, or wild and fancy-free? What about all those things. Do you wish for them too?"

"Yes, of course. Let's walk, the bicycle shop is just down the way," said Gabriel. "Yes, I want those things, but I want us to be equal with no jealousy: jealousy kills."

"A little jealousy can spark passion, you know," said Sydney glancing over with a knowledgeable slight of the eyes.

"No, I didn't know that. So what? Are you going to be my teacher? Professor Sydney, I like that. What do you think," asked Gabriel as he felt a little heat under his collar from the fruit of his thoughts?

"Are you implying I've been around the block a time or two? I'm no hussy, you know," said Sydney stopping and placing her hands on her hips and putting forth one leg slightly as to show comic disbelief.

"No! I didn't mean that. I know you're not a hussy, I mean, well I'm going to shut up now," said Gabriel laughing but half-serious.

"Good! Now take me to get a bicycle," said Sydney, the two now walking towards the shop that was just around the corner.

It only took a few minutes to reach the shop, and Gabriel said hello to one of his friends in the shop. He told him they were out of bicycles but said if you place me a free ad this month, I'll let you ride a new one. Gabriel told him she might bang it up a little. The shopkeeper told him the ad would be worth the money of the damage and more. They took the bicycle and walked it out. It was a cruiser-type bicycle, one that would be easy for Sydney to ride. They walked around the park a few minutes walking the bikes and trying to find a not so busy part of the park to begin her riding. After about ten minutes of talking and laughing, they stumbled upon the back gardens, and it wasn't too busy. He asked Sydney,

"You sure you're up to this?"

"I don't have a choice, do I," asked Sydney?

"Well, let me think... no, not really."

She put her hands on the handlebars and mounted the bicycle. She put her hand on the handlebars and mounted the bicycle. She seemed a little nervous, but she was smiling and laughing, perhaps a little embarrassed. Gabriel said,

"Now, just remember to keep your feet going, but by all means, keep steering."

She put her left foot on the pedal and began to push down, Gabriel told her,

"Now, the other, and don't forget to steer."

She began wobbling down the walkway, laughing, and trying to remember the coordination she had known so many years ago. She laughed and cried,

"I think I'm getting the hang of it. Look at me, Gabe!"

Gabriel mounted his Gavali and rode after her. Sydney was looking straight ahead until Gabriel pulled up beside her,

"It's fun, isn't it?"

"I can't believe you do something like this for a living, I mean just ride around and report on how fun things are," said Sydney.

"Well, actually now I'm kind of a desk jockey, not a field analyst, but anyway, I understand what you mean."

"I feel like a child, Gabe," said Sydney as she swung both legs and feet out from the bike and balanced on the seat carefully.

"If your childhood was great, then I'm happy for you," he said looking straight forward and pensive for the moment as they headed onward.

"That sounded rather jaded," said Sydney. She stopped her bicycle and looked at Gabriel and said, "What could have been so bad about your childhood that you would make a statement like that?"

"I have three years of cognitive life with my family in my memory, the rest is with the memories of another man's family, another man's joy. I lost my parents when I was very young, that's just something that takes a while to get over. Because of them, I became a solitary creature. I've lived alone ever since college. I never really dated anyone, and I became obsessed with my work. The Highlands gave me everything I could have asked for except a real family, and that's all I ever wanted. I guess I've just always wanted the security and love of a family."

Sydney said, "Let's ride." They got back on their bicycles and started rounding the park again. Sydney said, "Losing your parents must have been hard, but can't you be thankful for who you are now. Can't you let yourself be glad you're with me? That's all I want is for you to be happy, Gabe."

"I am with you," said Gabriel. "I guess I just don't want to mess things up with you. You're so wonderful and sweet and pretty, all I could ask for," They continued down the pathway for a few more minutes.

"Alright, Gabe, I'll bet you something. If you can beat me back to the bicycle shop, I'll bet you I can guarantee you and I will fall deeply in love and have a wonderful relationship," she said with a sideways smile.

"Alright, but you have a cruiser, and I'm on the fastest bicycle in the world," he boasted.

"I didn't finish," said Sydney. "I get a full two-minute head start, so you'd better ride fast, little boy."

"I'm still going to win," said Gabriel. "Alright on my mark you go, Okay. One, two, three, go!"

Sydney started with a slight wobble but straightened it out in a few yards. She seemed to be going at a medium pace at first and then picked up speed. He watched her go down the path, and he waited for 1:50, 51, 52, 53, 54, and on fifty-nine he mounted the bicycle and was off. He knew a shortcut through the park since he had made so many routes in his youth, and he made it to the shop in four and a half minutes. He walked into the shop and told the shopkeeper about what was going on. He hid in the back of the store. In a few minutes, Sydney came riding around the corner and stopped in front of the shop. The shopkeeper walked out and began talking to Sydney.

"Did you hear about the bicycle crash a few minutes ago?"

"What," she said abruptly and with great concern.

"Yeah, that guy on the touring bicycle got hit by a car. They said he was quite in a hurry and didn't look both ways across the street. I just had to call the ambulance."

"You can't be serious? Oh my goodness, it had to be Gabe," said Sydney looking frantic. "He could be seriously hurt."

She began trying to pay the man for the time on the bicycle, but he would not take the money. She became frantic near tears. Suddenly, Gabriel stepped out from behind the curtain at the shop and laughed, and began pointing at Sydney. She threw her hands in the air and started cussing,

"How could you do that to me, you heartless beast!"

"I'm sorry, ma'am, but I believe I won the bet, you owe me a lifetime of happiness," said Gabriel smiling with a slight blush.

She was still in disbelief but said, "Fine, perhaps you won the bet Mr. Liden, but you'll get no love from me today."

"Sydney, I'm sorry," said Gabriel, "It was only a joke, forgive me."

"You scared me," said Sydney. "You won the bet but broke my heart."

"How can I mend it," asked Gabriel with his right hand on his heart?

"Chocolate! Yes, you must buy me chocolate. It's the only way to mend a girl's broken heart," said Sydney.

"Then chocolate you shall have, love and my eternally devoted heart," said Gabriel. "I know the best chocolatier, just down the street. You can have all you desire."

The two walked from the shop down the avenue to a corner bistro. They sat and Sydney looked at the menu for a moment looking at all the chocolate desserts.

"If you'd like, they even have regular chocolate pieces for sale," said Gabriel with a smile. They left their seats and went to the glass display. There were chocolate-covered raspberries, strawberries, and even chocolate flowers. Sydney looked excited. She smiled and turned to Gabriel and said,

"Whatever you'd like, Gabe, you pick. I'll be at the table."

Sydney returned to the table and waited for her date. Gabriel was smart and ordered one of each so she could have them all. The chocolates were not cheap, but Gabriel made a good salary now, and he wished to spoil her. He returned to the table and waited for the myriad of chocolates to appear.

They ordered drinks and began talking. Gabriel asked how her day was, the closing, and the showing of the home. She told of a tiring yet productive day, but that it seemed to be ending quite nicely. She said, well except for her near heart attack, of course. Gabriel apologized again, and just as their drinks arrived, so did their feast of sweetness. Sydney said,

"Boy, you know how to win a girl's heart, don't you?"

Gabriel was proud of his thoughtful purchase, and the two ate aplenty, gorging themselves on the delicacies. Gabriel grabbed the chocolate covered strawberry and fed it to Sydney,

"Oh, it's sweet and tart, but I like it. Give me another."

He chose one that was visibly a filled piece, but he did not know with what. "A surprise for both of us," said Gabriel. He grabbed the piece of candy delicately, a little of the chocolate getting on his hands, and fed it to her. She took a moment and said,

"Yes, caramel," she said. "Here, you try a little of it."

Gabriel took the chocolate and took a small bite. He enjoyed the sweetness a lot, and the two kept eating the candy and drinking their drinks until the sun went down. They both felt a little bit of a sugar rush from the candy but decided to leave the bistro and go to the heart of the city. They hit the streets, walking with his bicycle and talking all along the way, and the conversation never ceased. When they reached the heart of the city Gabriel and showed her all the sites as they walked along.

"You make me feel young and at ease, Gabe," said Sydney. "You have a genuine honesty about you, and I feel because you have such a good ear, I could tell you anything. Why don't you tell me something, Gabe, your deepest darkest secret, something about your past?"

"My deepest darkest secret, huh," said Gabriel

"Yeah," said Sydney.

"I think there's something that pertains to you directly, actually," said Gabriel with candid eyes and looking rather shy.

"Something that pertains to me, huh."

"Yeah, see, I've never been very good with women."

"Uh, huh... Go on."

"Well, to tell the truth, I've never actually been with a woman," said Gabriel under his breath.

"So, you're a virgin," said Sydney calmly.

"Yes."

"Gabe, I think that's wonderful, and it explains a lot about you, don't be ashamed."

"I'm not, but how's that wonderful?"

"When I'm with you, I can feel you want to be with me, have my company, not my body alone. I can feel your passion and that you want to please me, but I feel you hold my respect above anything. This is not a conquest for you, Gabe. I can tell that."

"Well, what about you, Sydney, do you have experience?"

"I've had one partner my entire life, and I waited until I thought I was getting married to make that leap. In the end, my partner and I went separate ways because he was scared of marriage. He led me to believe otherwise to get me to be with him in that way. So, the answer is I have some experience, but not a lot. I've dated some but nothing serious. Does that put you at ease?"

"It makes me want to kill this dastardly fellow."

"Get in line. Look, the fact that you've never done certain things makes you even more of a catch, Gabe. It doesn't detract from your package as a whole. In fact, with you, I think it strengthens what you have to offer."

"Thanks, that means a lot. Just know that I've always wanted to wait until I found the right woman. I'm kind of old-fashioned that way. I hope that doesn't deter you from going forward. Anyway, along with that particular subject, my place is only a block from here. Would you like a cup of tea? I have some good herbal, and it won't keep you up."

"Good move, but how do you know I don't want to stay awake?"

"Let's say it's a good guess."

They continued walking down the street until they reached his building. The two entered and went up the elevator to his floor. They walked down the narrow hallway to his apartment and put the key in and turned the lock. He opened the door and allowed her to step in first. She saw the view and was amazed.

"No wonder you've stayed here all these years."

Gabriel began lighting his new candles. He turned off the lights for the metropolis lights were coming in from the window and illuminated the loft perfectly. Gabriel went to the kitchen and began boiling water in the kettle. Sydney sat down on the sofa and made herself comfortable, still admiring the view. Gabriel walked out of the kitchen of the loft and sat down in a large comfortable chair that he had loved for years. Sydney looked over at him and said,

"Why so far away, come closer. I won't bite."

Gabriel calmly got up from the chair and moved across to the sofa. He sat down, and she said, "Can I lean on you?"

Gabriel was scared and calm and excited all at once. She leaned against him and let out a sigh. He placed his arms around her and began touching the outside of her arm. She nestled into his chest, and they started talking about a lot of things. She began talking about her childhood in the Metropolis Girls School. The kettle whistled and she told him that she didn't really come up for the tea. Gabriel nervously sat her up from her nestled position, turned her in front of him, and grabbed her hand gently. He pulled her hand up and gave it a sweet, delicate kiss. Gabriel had become nervous. He took his other hand and, with the back of it, gently caressed her cheek. He took that same hand and placed his open palm on her other cheek and then down to her chin. They both leaned in and touched their lips to one another, kissing ever so gently. She gave a little smile and a slight satisfied noise. Her eyes, still closed, just letting him know to keep going. He went toward her a second time and kissed her lips, gently touching her tongue. His body was trembling. She could feel it, so she asked,

"Do you feel comfortable, you're shaking."

"I've never felt better," said Gabriel interlocking his fingers with hers.

They gently touched and kissed for a moment, both feeling warm inside. He stroked her hair and said, "That's enough for tonight," and he pulled away.

She laughed gently and said, "You've done that before."

Gabriel laughed quietly and said, "I'm a virgin, not an idiot."

"We should do that again sometime soon Gabe; I liked that," said Sydney pulling her locked fingers upward and separating their palms until she kissed his hand and let go.

"They'll be plenty later."

"When's later, Gabe," she said playfully.

"Not now, later. Please don't tempt me, you're too adorable. It's like a dream that you're here with me. I don't want you to leave, so just lay with me for a while."

The two of them laid down on the bed and embraced each other. Both thought about a lot of things, the future, the past, and of course, the present moment. Eventually, the two fell asleep on the bed holding each other, thinking of one another.

A good while passed as they slept groggily and eventually, Sydney awoke. She looked at the clock and it was five in the morning. She carefully woke Gabriel and told him she was calling a cab. Gabriel gave her the address half asleep, and he got up off the sofa. He told her he would get her a cab in the morning if she stayed, but she needed to make it to work early in the morning.

Gabriel and Sydney waited for a while and the call came from the cab. They both headed to the door and down the hallway and to the elevator. The two exited to the street where the cab was waiting. Gabriel gave a short sleepy, intimate kiss, and Sydney was off to uptown. Gabriel made his way back up to his loft. He set his alarm for a few hours and was off to sleep. Goodnight you two...

Chapter 9

Falling In Love

Gabriel woke the next day and was at work by nine, busy, and thinking of Sydney. He made a call to her mid-day just to make sure she was okay. She was loving on the phone, beyond smitten, and on a pathway to happiness. He finished the day and rode home as he usually would. The two talked on the phone and agreed to meet that coming Saturday and they would eat a nice meal at Sydney's place uptown.

Friday seemed to drag, and work seemed tedious. He did his job the best he could, considering he was blooming with emotions. Gabriel made it through the day and night, occasionally talking to Sydney before going to bed. He went for a Saturday morning ride to clear his mind, and the city looked beautiful. Everything seemed to look perfect, everything felt amazing. He was sure he must be in love, but he shouldn't tell her. He thought it might scare her off. Deep down, he knew she felt the same, so he rejoiced and finished his ride. He got home and called her and told her he would be there by six-thirty. Gabriel showered and readied himself for an intense evening.

He hailed a cab at six-ten and was off to the uptown area. He asked the driver to stop off at the nearest florist so he could get Sydney some flowers. He went into the florist and thought for a moment. He thought red roses were a little overdone, and yellow might give her the wrong idea. So, he bought a large bouquet of Gerber daisies just to be safe. A few minutes and he was back in the cab and off down to Virginia Ave. He did not want to be late, but there was construction on Commons; they just had to wait. Eventually, they got around the road work, and they made it to Sydney's house with only a few minutes to spare. He knocked on the door, and Sydney, dressed to the nines, opened the door and invited him inside.

"You're looking handsome, yet casual today," said Sydney looking him up and down.

"I didn't think a suit was proper for the occasion, so business casual it was," said Gabriel. "Forgive me, something smells wonderful. I can't wait to eat."

"That's actually for my other boyfriend Gabe; he's coming over at nine. I have a frozen dinner for you," said Sydney looking very serious.

"What other boyfriend? Wait, you're kidding, right," said Gabriel looking concerned.

"Maybe, maybe not Gabe," said Sydney with a deadpan face.

"Hey, you're creeping me out, you're kidding. Hey, stop looking like that."

"There's no one else, Gabe, don't be so uptight," said Sydney laughing at Gabriel's face of disgust. "Come on, let's go eat."

"Don't do that to me Sydney. You know no guy thinks that's funny. Guys don't like it when you make jokes about other guys," said Gabriel, half smiling.

They walked into the arched hallway adorned with very tasteful artwork, Gabriel thought. She said, "This is the living room and to the right, the formal dining room. Come on, Gabe, a little farther," said Sydney playfully and motioning with her right index finger. She walked a little more and said, "This is the den, this is where I do most of my reading, and every once and a while, I watch a little television. Oh, and over there is the bathroom in case you need it. Let's go back to the kitchen, Gabe."

They walked the rest of the way to the back of the house and to the kitchen. Gabriel asked, "What is that smell?"

"Beef tenderloin," said Sydney.

"I tried a tenderloin at my house once, but I'm afraid it didn't turn out so well; I overcooked it. Don't get me wrong I don't like it too rare, that upsets my stomach, but medium, medium well is perfect."

"Well, this one is almost done, so would you like to carve the meat, or shall I?"

"By all means, this is your show. I'm just going to sit and enjoy."

"A true gentleman," said Sydney sarcastically. "Why don't you make yourself useful and fix us something to drink. I always keep a good bottle of wine around for just such an occasion. Try the cab. Would you like to open it, or do you want me to do that too?"

"I think the wine is fitting, but just one glass for me," said Gabriel as he reached for the bottle in the wine rack.

He had a little trouble with the cork because he didn't do these sorts of things often. Nonetheless, Sydney carved the meat, and Gabriel poured the wine. They moved into the formal dining room where Sydney had set some candles before he got there. She lit them and brought the rest of the meal in from the kitchen. They sat at one end of the large glass table sitting directly across from one another. The walls were a light blue/grey with neutral curtains and two windows looking out towards the street. Gabriel looked around and was a little jealous of the space she had. But the meal smelled wonderful and hearty so they began with the delicacy and the side dishes, enjoying the meal, and Gabriel said, "I've never thought medium temperature could taste so tender."

They drank their wine and talked over the beautiful meal. The meat was starting to get cold because the two of them were so engrossed in their conversation. It was good anyway, they both thought. Eventually, they finished their wine and food, and Gabriel began to clean. He cleared the table and asked, "Are we having dessert, if not we could walk down and get some coffee. There's a coffee house only about five blocks from here."

"Yes, Gabe, I know, I live here, remember. But no, there is no dessert, that's not really my forte. I'm a meat and potatoes kind of girl, and fondue too, of course,"

Gabriel, a little intoxicated laughed and said, "Look, fried meat and vegetables can be very romantic. You know, especially when you leave the place with the smell of grease and cheese on your clothes and in the air."

Sydney laughed and thought for a moment and said, "Coffee would be wonderful, my treat. Let's go."

The two left out of Sydney's home and to the left down Virginia Avenue walking at a leisurely pace. They talked about a lot of things those first few blocks. They made it to the café and he looked at the host and said,

"A table for two. I'm feeling good tonight. What about you?"

"Perfect. I'll follow your lead."

They sat down at the table and ordered two glasses of water. The two looked at the menu of coffee drinks. Gabriel liked espresso a lot but thought just a café au lait would be good. Sydney ordered a coffee press. They received their coffee, "Gabe, umm, what'd you do this morning," asked Sydney?

"I actually went for a brief ride around town. I felt so good, considering the last week, so I went to all four parts of town. I even rode by the Boys School."

"Oh, really! Has it changed much?" Sydney grabbed his hand, assuring him that everything was going well. "I haven't been to The Girls School in a while. You didn't happen to ride by it, did you?"

"I did. They're building some type of new auditorium or something. It looks like a big venture," said Gabriel sipping on his café au lait. They talked about life, love, and work for about an hour, slowly drinking their coffee. Sydney chimes in after a long pause in the conversation,

"Gabe?"

"Yes, Sydney."

"You want to get a cab and go back to my house and finish this conversation? You might be put a little more at ease," said Sydney looking lovingly in his eyes and grabbing his hand again.

"Okay, but this is on me."

"Okay, but just this once, Gabe," said Sydney grabbing her things.

Gabriel paid the bill, and they were out the front door to the taxi stand just down the street. They made it back to Sydney's house, continuing their conversation. After about an hour she got up from one of the chairs in the living room and said, "I haven't shown you the rest of the house."

She grabbed his hand and walked him to the stairwell. They began climbing the stairs. They reached the landing at the top and turned to the left. They started down the hall and to the right was her office, one window overlooking the pristine back-yard, the other to the neighbor's house. There was a bedroom to the left she pointed out and another just down the hall on the left. But she pointed out the back bedroom, which was the master. They entered the door on the right, and Gabriel saw a queen size bed with large posts and curtains all around. The curtains were pulled back, and it was adorned with pillows along with the headrest of the bed. She showed him to the bathroom where he found a large claw foot tub and a separate shower. There was a large vanity, along with an antique full-length mirror. He thought to himself, and this is much more adult than my loft. Sydney said, "Come see how comfortable the bed is."

Gabriel was led by one hand to the large curtained bed where they sat and talked for a moment. Gabriel asked,

"Are you trying to seduce me?"

"I would never do such a thing, but if you wanted to kiss me, you could."

The wine was playing a part in her playfulness, as it was with Gabriel. He reached over and gently kissed her, and she said, "More, please." He gently kissed her again, both settling on the bed. Sydney threw the pillows onto the floor, and the two began exploring one another. Sydney said, "Stop me if you feel uncomfortable. I won't be upset."

They continued for a while, Gabriel brushing his hands against her body and continuing to kiss her delicate neck. After a few minutes of restrained enthusiasm, Sydney pulled away and stopped Gabriel, and said, "Maybe we should stop. I know I told you to stop me if you feel uncomfortable, but I don't think we should be drunk the first time, I'm sorry."

"It's okay. I'm pretty sure I would have stopped myself in a few minutes, so don't worry," said Gabriel lifting himself up from their sublime position and sitting off to one side. He straightened his hair and gave a loving kiss on the lips to assure her everything was okay.

"So, you're not mad. I didn't mean to lead you on."

"If I expected something from you, then you would have been leading me on. I only expect things to take their course, naturally. What do you say we just lay here and talk, okay?" said Gabriel with a slight smirk on his face.

"Thank you, Gabe, just for being who you are," said Sydney as she laid back on the remaining two sleeping pillows. Gabriel pulled himself around to the other side of the bed and grabbed her hand and kissed it. He brushed her hair off her brow and kissed it as well. They both got comfortable and talked about everything they could think of until an hour had passed. Gabriel said,

"Perhaps we should call it a night?"

"Doing this makes me special and kind of tingly inside, but I understand," said Sydney.

"Well, I'm glad something got tingly inside," said Gabriel with another deviant smirk.

"Hey! That's not fair. You said you would have stopped yourself," said Sydney laughing in disbelief.

"You know I'm just kidding, but I do have to go," said Gabriel as he started his way off the bed. "Walk me out? I can grab a cab down on the corner of Commons, no need to call one."

"But I don't want you to go yet," said Sydney sitting up on the bed.

"Come on, we'll go out a couple of times this week, I promise," said Gabriel putting on his shoes. "Actually, we'll get together as many times as you want next week, you choose the days."

"Monday through Sunday, how's that sound," asked Sydney?

"You know I still have to work Monday through Friday," said Gabriel. "Come on, let's go."

Sydney, under protest, got up from the bed and walked with Gabriel down the stairs and to the front door. She slowly kissed him on the lips and told him to be careful. He turned around, made a left out of the front yard. He looked back to see Sydney waving, and they agreed upon a call tomorrow. He walked the two houses up to Commons and hailed a cab.

He made it home around midnight and got ready for sleep. He didn't set his alarm and was off to sleep. Sydney went to sleep that night dreaming of her new infatuation, but she had to be at work in the morning. Her alarm was set for early in the morning, and she made herself get some sleep. Until tomorrow you two...

Chapter 10

A Gift

Gabriel woke the next day and went about his day as he usually did. He called Sydney that afternoon and left a message asking her if she wanted to get together in the next day or two. The week continued and eventually ended. He went to the grocery store and got home around six and began fixing himself a light dinner. Sydney called around seven-thirty, explaining how she had had a long day but was looking forward to a gentle bath in her tub. They talked for about an hour until finally, Sydney said it was bath time. They hung up the phone, and each went about the rest of their night thinking of one another.

The next day came and they met at the museum and walked through for a couple of hours exploring the modern exhibit. They went back to Gabriel's loft after and ate a midevening light dinner. When they got to the loft, they settled in and sat up and talked for a couple of hours. They spoke of growing up as school children. Gabriel unabashedly spoke about his youth but still hid his lineage beginning in the outer parts. They also talked about Sydney's parents and how much she loved them and, most of all, their feelings for one another.

They began strong and would continue that way for the next few months until the holiday season came around. The two put up festive décor at Sydney's house and exchanged gifts for the first time on the great holiday. Sydney got Gabriel some bicycle accessories, and Gabriel got Sydney some clothes from Lordes, including some intimate apparel that surprised her. This was a momentous night for the couple, a coming of age, so to speak, for they both told one another that they loved each other. They spent the night of the great holiday exploring each other's boundaries and being playful with one another.

The holiday came and went, and the new year came. The two spent the night in the heart of the city as he had done as a child, and they kissed at the new year strike. This was a first for Gabriel, and Sydney was happy to make the memory with him. They walked that evening from the festivities to his house, spending the evening together, getting ever closer to fully embracing their physical relationship together.

January passed by quickly, for they were both working hard at work and staying up late with each other. The two had not argued the entire time they had been together and saw it as a sign and a testament to their relationship. They began spending every waking hour together after work and into the late-night hours. Eventually, the all-hearts day came around, and Gabriel planned an elaborate night. They started the night out at the chocolatier and had some desserts just to get her tempted for the evening. Next, they went on a horse and carriage around the heart of the city. Sydney remarked that she thought he was a better tour guide of the area than the driver. Gabriel laughed, grabbed her by the hand, thanked her, and kissed her on the lips.

He had the carriage drop them off at Gabriel's house, and he had a candlelight dinner waiting to be finished in a few short minutes after they arrived. He chose beef tenderloin and made sure he cooked it medium. They finished off the night before bed with Gabriel giving her a gentle rub of her shoulders. She turned and looked over her left shoulder, turned slightly and they began kissing one another. They professed their love for one another, and the night continued until almost four in the morning.

The next few months passed much the same as usual, the two never going out with other couples or even seeing their co-workers outside of work, only engaging each other. They would occasionally go to a movie or spend a rare evening in a bookstore just perusing the new arrivals. The two joked about spending the rest of their lives together, and Gabriel began pondering it seriously. He had never loved anyone as much as he loved Sydney, not even his parents. Sydney taught him to be a different kind of man. He felt his inner child was free for the first time in his entire adult life. Gabriel had become a confidant, also a student in the ways of the heart. Mostly, he had become her companion and friend throughout the days and nights. He taught her much of the same, except he showed her the beauty of innocence again. Sydney was perfectly content in their exploration. Gabriel held back some, for he knew he wanted her to be his wife, but it was too early, he thought.

The summer came, and it was a hot, sultry summer. The two were often found walking through the gardens in the park and even attending a baseball game or two that year. But the summer began creeping by, and Gabriel's birthday was approaching. Sydney told him she had a surprise for him, but he asked that she let him take her out that day; Gabriel planned to ask her to marry him.

The day of his birthday came around, and he was a little nervous, he knew they were in love, but would she say yes. He had purchased a ring, a two-karat princess cut ring, fitting for a princess, he thought. He didn't have to work that day, nor did Sydney, so they met and had an early breakfast. They enjoyed the morning together just walking around the shopping district in midtown, and they decided to part ways until about six that night. Sydney told him he was going to be so surprised, but she told him he had one guess, and she would tell him if he was close. He guessed a new seat for my bicycle. She told him he was close, but he would have to wait until he got to her house at six. Gabriel put her in a cab. She was off to get ready for the evening's festivities. Gabriel was having thoughts of doubt, not of his own but envisioning Sydney's answer being maybe, or a decisive no. Nonetheless, he went back to his home and began preparing for the evening.

He got his surprise ready and made sure he had the ring still and showered for the night's plans. He was ready by five fifteen, grabbed his things, and went to hail a cab. Luckily one drove by right as he was walking out. He held up his hand and the cab driver asked where he was going? He told him the corner of Virginia and Commons. He stopped at the old florist he had gone to so many times and got her some spider lilies. They were back in the car and to their corner by ten until six. He was let out on the corner and walked the two houses down and rang the bell. Sydney screamed something to the effect that she was not ready. He stood outside for a moment or two. Eventually, she came to the door dressed to kill, and Gabriel's jaw dropped when he saw her. He gave her a huge kiss, and he walked in the front door. Sydney was extra excited, for she had his present to give him still. She asked him if he wanted it now or later, and of course, he said now.

She told him to wait in the hall, and she went back into the den and asked him to close his eyes. She came out and asked him to open his eyes. When Gabriel opened his eyes, he saw a Gavali bicycle, and he was speechless. He looked it over for a moment, but there was a problem. The bicycle she had purchased was way too small for him, but he didn't want to say anything. He went to give her an enormous jubilant hug, but she pulled away. He asked her what was wrong, and she said it is too small, isn't it? Gabriel said yes, being the honest man that he was. She told him to wait a moment, and she went in and wheeled out the second gift: his bicycle. He said you bought us matching Gavalis, but how? She explained that the million-dollar home she was closing on would easily cover the cost. She wanted to see the city the way he did. He had no idea what to say. He would be the envy of his magazine; two Gavali Touring bicycles. He really had no words, so he grabbed her and swung her around, and kissed her as thankfully as he possibly could.

She asked where they were going, and he had this month's issue of the Metro Cyclist, and he gave it to her. He told her to hold onto it. He wanted her to read his new article at dinner, it was pertinent to their evening. She put it in her purse, and they walked down the street and hailed a cab, and headed to midtown and One Midtown Avenue.

They drove up and the bellhops ran to their car. He told them there was no luggage; they were just eating dinner. One of the bellhops said something to the effect that it was never "just" eating dinner there, sir. They went in a revolving door and past the concierge and to the elevator. The restaurant was on the top floor of the hotel, one of the finest in the city. It overlooked the entire metropolis. They rode the glass elevator to the top floor, stepped out, and were captivated by the view immediately.

The host asked them their name and he found it on the reservation list. They were to be seated at seven but began talking at the bar.

"You said you had a surprise for me, but I bet it's not as good as mine," said Sydney placing her hand on his knees.

Gabriel put his right hand on his right pocket to make sure the ring was there and said,

"Maybe you want to read my new article now?"

"It can wait, I just want to stare at you. You're so beautiful Gabe," said Sydney looking lovingly in his eyes.

"And I've told you, you are the best-looking woman in town, and I meant that, love," said Gabriel starting to get nervous, just wishing she would pull out the magazine.

The seven o'clock hour came, and their table was ready, so they sat and got comfortable. The two ordered appetizers, then two entrées. They ate their salads and drank their wine for it was a special occasion. They finished their salads and went straight to the main course: lobster and filet mignon. They ate well, but Gabriel was so nervous. At one point she asked him if he was okay and of course, he said he was fine, but they finished their meal, and Gabriel said,

"Why don't you read my article now? I think you'll like it, read it aloud."

"Alright, Gabe. It's your birthday," said Sydney reaching for her purse.

She grabbed the magazine and said, "Ooh, a honeymoon issue through the far seas."

Gabriel had made a false copy just for Sydney to read. She began reading. The best honeymoon time is late summer. As she read, she came to a part that said, 'I went to the far seas with my wife in late summer.'

"You're not married, that's dishonesty," she said, laughing.

She kept reading. The story of my wife is that I asked her to marry me on my birthday at One Midtown Avenue. Gabriel reached in his pocket and grabbed and opened the ring. Sydney had a sudden realization. She paused for a moment,

"Are you asking me to marry you Gabe, is that what this is about? Are you actually," Sydney said with bridled excitement.

Gabriel got on his right knee and said, "Will you marry me, Ms. Sydney Bloomfield? Will you make me the happiest man in the world and be my wife?"

"I guess your surprise was bigger than mine. Of course, I'll marry you, Gabe," said Sydney looking near teary-eyed.

He placed the ring on her finger; it was a perfect fit. They both stood up and gave each other an emotional embrace and kiss, then Sydney sat in silence, smiling.

"What's wrong, you're quiet," asked Gabriel?

"I thought it would take you years to ask me. I wanted you to ask, but I did not know if you would. I am so excited. Let's get married tomorrow. I have never really wanted a big wedding. All we need is a priest. What do you think Gabe," asked Sydney twirling the ring around her finger?

"I was hoping you'd say that. We don't really have any friends, and both our parents are gone, so it only makes sense. The sooner, the better I say, I want to be with you," said Gabriel with a sigh of relief and an eased heart.

"Are we really going to the far seas metropolis," asked Sydney, giggling and fidgeting like a schoolgirl.

"Let's take next week off and go," said Gabriel. "Today is Friday we can get married tomorrow, pack on Sunday, and leave on Monday. How's that sound?"

"Perfect, let's pay the bill and get out of here. We'll go to the bistro and get some dessert, no wait this one's on me it's your birthday."

Sydney paid the bill, and they were off to celebrate the rest of the evening. The one thing Gabriel wanted more than anything in his life, he was finally going to get: his love Sydney. They left the restaurant and made their way to the bistro. Gabriel was relieved and excited. Sydney was glowing, looking at her ring and feeling youthful.

They hailed a cab and were at the bistro in no time. It was Friday night, so it was busy, but they were seated quickly and began planning the days ahead.

"Do you really want to get married tomorrow, you don't think that's too soon," said Sydney. "I want you, Gabe. We've held back for so long now. I just want to be with you."

"I know this doesn't happen to be the most romantic thing, but the only place we're going to find a priest at such short notice is in one of the churches downtown," said Gabriel stroking her hand. "I know it's not ideal, but if we're just looking for a short ceremony, we can probably get one for under four or five hundred dollars."

"If I had a justice of the peace, I'd marry you right now, Gabe," said Sydney. "Now that I know you've been thinking about this for a while, it makes me want to be with you, now. Let's just skip the dessert and go home. I hope you know I want you to come to my house to stay for good. Just think all those nights you've given me a bath or stayed over. That will be every night, Gabe, aren't you excited?"

"I'm ecstatic, love. If you want to go, we can. But we've waited for so long, let's just wait until tomorrow," said Gabriel grabbing and gently caressing her hand.

"I have the perfect dress in mind. Are your suits clean," asked Sydney? She started to get up from her seat, "Come on, Gabe, let's go. I know, can we go for a ride? Give me a tour."

Gabriel said, alright, and they both left their seats and headed for the door. There was a cab stand just down the street, and they got in and said, "Virginia and Commons." They met a little bit of traffic since it was Friday, but made it to their new home in under twenty minutes. They paid the cab driver and moved right along into Sydney's house. The bicycles were calling them. They changed clothes and Gabriel always kept extra riding gear around Sydney's house. Sydney put on a pair of jeans, for there was a slight chill in the air that night. They grabbed the bicycles and down the front walkway to Virginia Avenue. Gabriel asked,

"Where do you want to go, love?"

"Somewhere only you know," replied Sydney.

Gabriel had just the place in mind. They got to the street, and Gabriel warned her that a geared bicycle was slightly different from the ones they had ridden before. Sydney mounted the seat and started on their journey. He led her to Commons and turned right. Sydney got the hang of the bicycle quickly, and they were off down the road.

"Be careful of traffic," he said. They continued on Commons talking the whole way until they reached Langley Avenue and turned left. Sydney didn't know, but they were heading towards the outer part of the city. Langley went straight to the outer parts and to the country. Sydney had no idea where she was going. She'd never seen the city in such a way, and she'd never been that far down Langley.

"My bottom hurts," cried Sydney from behind Gabriel.

"He laughed and said, "It's going to hurt tomorrow, too."

After about twenty-five minutes of riding, they reached the small overpass to which Gabriel had wanted to go. Sydney, tired and sore, rode up behind him and said,

"I feel like I'm about to be in a murder scene. Where are we?"

"Just wait," said Gabriel. "Be patient, love."

A few minutes went by, Sydney now wondering where he had taken her. Suddenly, a plane went overhead landing on the strip just beyond the overpass, Sydney was awestruck. She had only been on a plane a few times in her life, but she had never seen one fly so close. Gabriel said,

"We'll be here Monday if you still want to. I know your muscles hurt, and your legs are tired, but tell me you can appreciate this, and we'll marry tomorrow."

"Only you would know such a beautiful place, Gabe. I will marry you tomorrow, uptown, downtown, midtown, or the heart of the city, you pick the place," said Sydney walking over and giving him a passionate kiss and a hug.

They watched the planes come in, one about every five minutes or so at that hour of the night. A car would pass over the overpass, every now and then, but for the most part, they were alone. They sat for about an hour when Gabriel said they should probably leave since they had to ride back so far away. They watched one more plane come in, and Sydney said, "I still don't understand how such a beautiful man could have made it this far in his life, never to have landed a beautiful and compassionate woman."

"Everyone has a soul-mate, and everyone was meant to be with one person. I may have been shy until I was twenty-eight, and for a reason, I must have gone to that bar that night. There are no coincidences. I was meant to be with you, Sydney. It's my destiny, and yours to be with one another. I love you."

"I love you too, Gabe. Come on, let's go. Our time starts tomorrow," said Sydney.

They mounted their bicycles and started riding back to Sydney's house, soon to be Gabriel's home as well. On the way home, Sydney still complained that her seat still hurt, and Gabriel laughed and told her just to hold on. They eventually turned onto Commons and left onto Virginia, dismounting the bicycles and going inside. The two went inside and searched the computer for a chapel for tomorrow, and eventually found one. The Church of the Faith was located downtown almost across the street from Gabriel's old school. They went to sleep at midnight that night, hoping to get a good night's rest for the coming day would be a great day. They lay side by side, each taking the opportunity to love one another before the next morning. That night would be Gabriel's last night without the knowledge of true adult love. He fell asleep in Sydney's arms. Good luck and sleep well, you two...

Chapter 11

Commitments

They woke that morning with a great feeling of hope, for today would be a great day of joy. The two wrestled themselves from the bed and made it to the telephone to book an appointment with the church. After a few minutes on the phone and making times for both their license and ceremony, they got dressed and made it out for a small breakfast. Sitting at their favorite breakfast spot the two talked freely,

"At three-thirty, we'll be married, Gabe," said Sydney. "You still want to marry me, don't you, Gabe?"

"Of course, love and tomorrow we will make plans for the far seas, it's been a long time since I've been out of the metropolis. I believe the last time I was out of the city I was arrested with Arthur Highland."

"You were arrested with Arthur Highland, oh please do tell," said Sydney looking curiously interested at Gabriel.

"We actually went camping and had an argument. We went without Haw knowing. But on the way home, we had a bottle of alcohol with us in the car and got pulled over. I was driving, that's what got us into so much trouble. To make a long story short, Haw had to bribe us out of trouble," said Gabriel laughing.

"How come you never told me that story? Anyway, you never told me you knew how to drive," said Sydney pushing her food around her plate.

"Well, I didn't have my license, and I was only fifteen. I think Haw paid about two thousand dollars to the county patrol. That is how I started working for Haw. It was to repay the money. Then I just kept working through college, until I got my first job," said Gabriel looking intently at Sydney and still laughing a bit.

"Arthur didn't care you worked there, even though you guys had a falling out?"

"Haw was good to me, Arthur aside. Anyway, Arthur was off at school most of the time. Haw would have never done anything to hurt me. He gave me my first Gavali for goodness sake," said Gabriel eating his eggs and toast, watching his soon-to-be wife's every delicate move.

"Stop looking at me like that," said Sydney, slightly touching his hand in a joking manner.

"What? I want you, I'm sorry," said Gabriel leaning forward in his seat.

"You're embarrassing me, come on, let's finish and get out of here," said Sydney finishing her plate of food.

The two finished their food and got a cab back to the loft so Gabriel could get his attire for the day. While they were back at the loft, they booked a suite for the night at The Metropolitan Plaza, his home for so many years. They both retreated to Sydney's house for a little while to let them both get ready and make sure all was in order.

"Do you have your identification, love? You'll need two different forms of I.D., like a birth certificate and a license, or something like that," said Gabriel, carefully looking through some of her personal papers for her.

"Look in the third drawer. You'll find my birth certificate and Gabe?"

"Yes, love?"

"I'm going to change my name. I want to be Mrs. Sydney Liden. Will that make you happy?"

"Of course, but you know you don't have to. You could hyphenate or not take it at all, and that would be fine," said Gabriel, looking at her reflection from the hallway and hoping this was not all a dream.

"No! I've made up my mind. Mrs. Sydney Liden will suit me fine. Gabe?"

"Yes, love?"

Sydney stopped doing her hair and began speaking to Gabriel in an earnest voice. She turned from the reflection and looked him in the eye, "When will you move in?"

"After the honeymoon, of course. I don't have much, mainly a lot of cycling gear and suits. My furniture can be donated when I move. Of course, I'll be here the first-day possible."

"Once you're here, you can never leave, you know?"

"Why would I want to, love?"

"You're mine Gabe for all eternity."

"I don't think that would be long enough."

The two dressed for the occasion, not too fancy, but packed a bag for the night at the hotel. Two-thirty came around quickly, and Gabriel called for her to come; it was time. She stepped out of the back bedroom, and Gabriel was, once again, stunned; she was more beautiful and radiant than she'd ever been. He straightened his collar, held out his arm, and asked her to join him. They went to Sydney's car and started out on their way downtown. There shouldn't be any traffic, he thought, as Sydney pulled out of the driveway. They made their way to the hundredth and thirty-fourth street in under twenty-five minutes. They reached the church at five-after-three. Their license appointment was in ten minutes, so they paced around anxiously, awaiting their time. They went to the window inside the license office and spoke to the man inside.

"We have a three fifteen appointment and we're to be married at three-thirty. Is everything on schedule," asked Sydney nervously happy fumbling through her papers?

The peculiar man in the office, dressed in an old grey suit and ragged tie pushed up his glasses and said, "I don't know who told you about your appointment, but it takes fifteen to twenty minutes for the license to be processed."

"Oh..." said Sydney. "Well, are we at least on schedule still, sir?"

"The Church of the Spirit is always on time. The faith keeper is always on time," said the peculiar man from behind the window.

"Very well, we'll be patient then," said Sydney backing up from the window.

The man said, "We'll call you in approximately six minutes. You may have a seat."

Sydney turned around and sat next to Gabriel and held his hand. In approximately six minutes, the two were called to come back to receive their license. They signed a lot of paperwork, took a quick blood test, and at three-thirty-three the licensing officer said, "You're now married congratulations!"

"What about the ceremony in the church," asked Gabriel?

"The ceremony in the church is for your union with the keeper. The metropolis recognizes paper, not a holy union. We always recommend showing your faith in a ceremony, however. That way, the keeper knows you're married," said the officer. "Just go through those doors, and to the alter, I've already given your materials to the parish. Good luck!"

They went through the doors and into the chapel and were married by the keeper at three forty-five. They gave a short kiss and were off to the car to a ride to The Metropolitan Plaza, where they would finally consummate their marriage and begin their new relationship. They drove to the posh midtown, and to the plaza, and were met by the bellhops. The car was parked, and they checked in at the desk. The suite they wanted was being occupied, but they were given a suite on the twentieth floor. The bags were taken up to the room, and they left the desk and made it to the elevator. They got in and started the ride.

"Which suite are you going to," asked the elevator operator.

"I believe twenty-A," said Sydney looking at the room key.

"Oh, that has a beautiful view, very romantic. You guys married," asked the operator?

"About an hour ago, actually," said Gabriel.

"Congratulations, and welcome to The Plaza. We're at your floor now, you kids don't do anything I wouldn't do," said the operator.

They exited to the floor and found room twenty-A. They opened the door to a grand room with a single rose and a bottle of the finest champagne The Plaza had to offer. There was a note just next to the bottle, and Gabriel read it aloud:

"I make it a point to know who is staying at my hotel. When I was alerted you were coming and requesting a honeymoon suite, I figured congratulations were in order. I'm sure you have things to attend to, but take this bottle of Champagne as a gift from all of us at the hotel, and enjoy brunch compliments of us in the morning. To your lovely wife and to old times, Arthur."

Gabriel put down the note and motioned for his new wife to come here. He popped the champagne and they had a few glasses. They began exploring each other and never even made it to the bedroom. They made love for the first time in the great room of suite twenty-A, and it was nothing less than perfect, beautiful, loving, but also innocent and fun. They continued throughout the night, making love and indulging in each other. Eventually, the insatiable appetite for one another had calmed long enough for some food. They hadn't eaten since the morning. They ordered and ate the most elegant meal and continued loving one another for the rest of the night. By the end of the night, Gabriel and Sydney eventually fell asleep holding one another, complete and wholly in love with each other.

The morning came quickly, for they had fallen asleep late into the night. They made love then showered and headed for the city's best brunch compliments of Arthur Highland. They made a slow affair of the morning, enjoying the company of each other as spouses. They spoke casually as the brunch went on drinking champagne, "You're an amazing man, Gabriel," said Sydney, innocently playing with her food.

"I couldn't have asked for more my first time. You're not so bad yourself. I love you, but you already know that, don't you? I couldn't ask for anything else. Thank you," said Gabriel feeling confidant in their love, and now a man wholly in love with his soulmate.

"We don't have to go on the honeymoon tomorrow, Gabe. Why don't we get you moved in with your clothes and stuff tonight and just enjoy a week together? I feel travel would almost be bothersome. We can go later to the far seas. I just want to spend some time at home alone."

"If that's what you want, love. It'll probably take a few trips in your car. We could just get my clothes and toiletries tonight, and get a few trips in over the week."

"That sounds good, Gabe. I just want to be with you, however, wherever, whenever," said Sydney, staring at Gabriel with glossy eyes and a relaxed demeanor.

"Let's just finish this beautiful meal, and we'll take it slow, okay love."

"Yes, Gabe," said Sydney grabbing his hand from across the table.

They finished the meal and checked out of the hotel. They went to Gabriel's loft and gathered his necessities. They were off back to Sydney's and Gabriel's new home. It's kind of funny, had it not been for the death of Ignatious Hawthorne

Highland these two may have never met. Arthur had exceeded the middle, which he had planned all along. Now, Gabriel was holding true to his promise, to make it to the middle. He was now a resident of the uptown area. Hold Fast Gabriel...

Chapter 12

The Country

The two slept that previous night as lovers and best friends, now residents of the same abode. They spent the week riding around town just loafing around the house. They were getting used to one another's true living habits and just loving being with each other. Gabriel had found his soulmate, as had Sydney. They were both delighted in their new lives. They eventually went back to work, sharing their time after work and on the weekends, riding together throughout the city, and taking walks after work. For the most part, things seemed normal for the couple. The air was cold now, but everything seemed great until eventually, a few months had passed. Gabriel came home from work and found Sydney at the kitchen table with a box full of letters. He asked,

"What are these letters, love?"

"They came when I got home from work; they're letters to your parents," said Sydney, slowly sifting through the letters. "I read a few and the dates on the letters, but I noticed something strange. You said your parents died when you were six. These are well after you said they'd died. What's going on, Gabe? There is one that is not opened yet that is addressed to you. I'm asking what's going on Gabe, why are these letters here?"

Gabriel was curious himself. He knew most likely why they were there. Though his parents were probably still alive, there had been no contact for years. He did not know how to recant on his claim of their death. He grabbed the note and read it to himself. As he read, Sydney continued to question him. She seemed overly concerned. He finished the letter and handed it to her. She began reading,

Dear Gabriel,

We have not had contact in many years, but I wanted to explain why I sent you all these letters. Years ago, when your father could not afford to pay for your school, a man by the name of Ignatious Hawthorn Highland contacted us and told us he would be taking care of you. We wanted to answer your letters, but he advised us not to. All these years, he told us he would be in contact with us when we could contact you again. It has been many years, but we received a letter from him and his estate saying he had passed on, and it was okay to contact you now. We have been searching for you for some time now. Gabriel, your father is ill and doesn't have much time left. I'm not sure when this letter will get to you, but I wish for you to see him one last time before he passes on. We don't have a phone anymore, so please write back soon.

Your Mama,

Anne

Sydney was taken aback. She did not know what to say. She did not know whether to be angry or give him a moment. So she just stood up and kissed his forehead.

"Why didn't you tell me, Gabe," asked Sydney, looking very concerned.

"What, tell you I'm a poor child from the outer parts? They abandoned me when I was just a boy," Gabriel said, near tears in his eyes.

"You think I wouldn't love you because of where your parents are from? You should have told me; no secrets, Gabe. Now that it's out in the open, what are you going to do about the letter? I think you should go and see him. I think we should go and see him. Show them what a good man you've become. Write your mother back and tell her we'll be there next week. I hope it's not too late, Gabe," said Sydney, gathering all the letters.

"What am I supposed to say to them when we get there? H, thanks for all the years I had without you," said Gabriel pacing around the room.

"Gabe, they're still alive, be happy about that. You have a chance to reconnect with them if only for a short time. Write the letter, Gabe," said Sydney getting up from the table and grabbing his hand. "Sit and write, Gabe. I promise you'll feel better."

Gabriel grabbed a piece of paper and began writing. He began writing all he had wished to say those early years and beyond. He told his mother he would be there within the week and his new wife with him. He signed it coldly, Gabriel Liden.

He mailed the letter, and he and his wife talked about everything she should have known. She assured him she did not care about his humble background. He was a man of truth and honor now. She loved him, and that was all he needed to know. They cooked dinner, and Gabriel found himself looking through the letters.

"This is the letter I sent them when Haw bought me my first bicycle. And this one, the last one when I graduated from The Boys School. I sent so many, every winter holiday, every birthday, thinking they just didn't care. To think that Haw was behind all the non-communication," said Gabriel " I'd really like to see the letter he sent and why didn't she send it to me. I don't know Sydney, what am I supposed to say to them?"

"Look, let's just take the next few days easy. It's Sunday the letter will be there by Wednesday. We can go on Saturday, and you'll think of what to say. It will come to you. Now, let's clean the dishes and make an early night of it. It's been a tough day," said Sydney starting to clean the kitchen table off.

They finished the dishes and did as they said they would and made an early night of it. Gabriel slept restlessly, getting up several times to wash his face, seemingly feeling lost. But the morning came, and they both made it to work. They went to work, but Gabriel wasn't necessarily in his best form. He was a little preoccupied.

The next few days passed in a haze; Wednesday, Thursday, and Friday until Saturday came. Two packed the car and set the GPS system. They headed out of town to unfamiliar territory, Gabriel still not knowing what to say when they arrived. The car ride seemed long, neither Sydney nor Gabriel spoke. Sydney was worried about Gabriel, and Gabriel was worried about whether he would lose his temper. Would all the feelings of the last number of years come out?

Suddenly, Gabriel said to Sydney, "I can't do this. I don't think I can do this."

"Gabe, you already told her you were coming; there's no turning back now. You need to do this. If you don't, your entire life, you'll wonder what could have been. Just calm down, Gabe, you're fine. Besides, I'd like to meet them. I am your wife now if you'll remember."

"You are right, love. I'm just acting stupid. Things will be fine." He calmed his breath and turned towards the window. He watched as they drove down Langley towards the outer parts and to uncertainty.

They continued the car ride, eventually entering the far outer parts. They drove through the drab countryside for what seemed like hours and hours. Gabriel had no memory of the road but he had been down that path before. Eventually, they made it to Liden Farms, winter now. The hands were not tending to the crops, nor were there many memories to be remembered. They drove down the driveway to the house, and just as they were parking the car, a withered older woman walked out, looking uncomfortable in the cold. She walked down the stairs, Gabriel barely remembered and walked towards the car. Gabriel stepped out, Sydney following suit, and they walked towards Gabriel's mother. She reached out her arms and said, "After all these years, my baby returns home, safe and sound. When you went away, I didn't know you were leaving, but it is so good to see you now, love."

"Hello mother, this is my beautiful wife, Sydney. As I told you, we were married just a few months ago."

"It's wonderful to meet you, Mrs. Liden," said Sydney hugging Gabriel's mother.

"Call me Anne, love. Come on in it's freezing out you two, let's go inside."

Anne grabbed Sydney's hand and led her up the stairs. They entered the home, and Gabriel had a rush of emotion. He remembered the inside of the home quite well. There was the smell of a pie being baked and the looming smell of a pot roast. Anne said,

"I fixed your favorite pie, apple I believe it was."

"Truthfully, mother, I don't remember, it was so long ago. Where's father," asked Gabriel?

"You said in your letter you wanted to talk to him. I'm afraid his words will be very few now. He is very ill," said Anne sitting down in her favorite chair. "Please won't you two sit and make yourselves comfortable."

The two sat on the old ragged couch, and Sydney grabbed Gabriel's hand and gave him a reassuring pat on their coupled hands. Anne fidgeted for a moment or two. Gabriel began feeling very uncomfortable. From the backroom Gabriel heard a faint mutter, Gabriel jumped to his feet and said, "Good. Is he awake? Can we talk now?"

"Gabriel, he is not well. Perhaps he cannot speak," said Anne stepping in front of the hallway entrance.

"He didn't give me a choice when I was a child, and I won't give him a choice now," said Gabriel walking through the archway and down the hallway. "Which room is it? Father, where are you?"

He heard a faint calling from the last room on the left and ducked in. His emotions were running high, his heartbeat rising by the second. When Gabriel entered the room, he found a man beaten down by the world, broken and scarred from a long life of manual labor and tobacco use. He called to Gabriel,

"Come here, boy," he said in a raspy cough.

"I'm no boy, father. I'm a man now. I've got a wife and a home of my own now," said Gabriel sternly.

"You know, I've read every one of your letters a hundred times. I knew what the first week of your schooling was like, and I knew the last, but one day you stopped," said James slowly with his intermittent cough. "Did you receive my gift, son?"

"I don't believe you ever sent me a gift except for the memory of you leaving after my first year," said Gabriel standing at the edge of the bed, wondering what gift he'd ever received from him.

"You know, your bicycle. I couldn't afford a car, but through your letters, you said you loved to bicycle, so I bought you the best money could buy, I saved for years for that bicycle," said James looking for his son's approval.

"You're telling me you bought that Gavali for me, not Haw? There's no way you bought that. I must have described it in one of my letters."

"No, no son, it was me," said James coughing. "Since I did such a nice thing for you, maybe you will help me out now."

"I knew it! You wanted something from me all the time. What father do you need, money? What is it," said Gabriel, shouting at his father!

"I'm going to need you to take in your mother when I pass. She can't run this place on her own," said James staring into Gabriel's cold eyes.

"I fucking knew it! I knew you had an agenda," said Gabriel shouting. "The only reason you sent me to school was to make your own life better, you selfish bastard. I wouldn't take either of you in to save my life. Just waltz back in... NO! I REFUSE!"

"Gabriel," yelled James from his bed as Gabriel started to leave the room. "Gabriel, please."

Gabriel stormed out of the room, turned, and made his way down the hall where his mother met him. "Gabriel, you must understand I have nowhere to go."

"It is of no concern to me. Sydney, we're leaving, grab your coat," said Gabriel reaching for the door. "LET'S GO NOW!"

Gabriel had never raised his voice to Sydney, so she knew something was very wrong. She grabbed her things and headed out the door with Gabriel. Anne was close behind, begging him to consider it. He was her only hope.

"Why don't you call Liza? I'm sure she has a home for you," said Gabriel as he got into the car.

"Liza died of pneumonia when she was fifteen, Gabriel. There is nowhere else to go," begged Anne stepping out swiftly into the cold.

Sydney got in the driver's seat, and they began pulling out of the driveway. Gabriel yelled, "I know a man named Arthur Highland, he lives in the metropolis, he deals with charity cases, well at least he did mine. Good luck!"

Sydney drove away concerned, not knowing what was happening. She turned to him and asked, "What did he say, Gabe? What sent you so far off?"

"He wants me to take in my mother when he passes, THAT RAT BASTARD," screamed Gabriel. "I should have known they were up to something. He had a plan to start with, and he had a plan to end it all Man, I'm a fool. Oh, by the way, thank you for the Gavali because I'm throwing my first one away."

"Gabe, what are you talking about?"

"My first Gavali was a gift from THAT man. I don't ever want to see it again. Haw, I thought Haw was kidding when he said the bicycle was from the holiday keeper. Hell, Haw didn't buy it. Let's just get out of here, Sydney. I need out of here."

Sydney didn't say a word, she just pointed the car in the right direction. She didn't know what to say. She loved him, but for the first time in their relationship, she didn't know how to comfort him. Gabriel just stared out the window and sank into a deep depression.

They drove through the farm country for about an hour. All of a sudden, they came around a corner and there was nothing but cows in the way. Gabriel sprung up and braced himself while Sydney hit the brakes. There was no avoiding it. They slammed violently into the herd, one animal directly into the front of the car. They both lost consciousness, and there was no doubt that both sustained massive injuries. The car had been stopped dead in its tracks: totaled. Help is on the way, Gabriel...

Chapter 13

A Phone call

"Mr. Liden, can you hear me? Mr. Liden" called a voice. He heard the voice and began to stir himself. He was not sure where he was, but the voice called again, "Mr. Liden, my name is Dr. David Wallace, can you hear me?"

"What," said Gabriel, trying to understand the stimuli around him.

"Mr. Liden, you're in the metropolis Mercy Hospital intensive care ward. Can you hear me?"

"Yes," said Gabriel. "Where am I? What happened?"

"You and your wife were in an accident in the outer parts. You were flown in by helicopter to the hospital. It's common to have some memory loss in an accident such as the one you were in," said Dr. Wallace.

Gabriel tried sitting forward, but he was in great pain. He looked down at his body and limbs, only to discover he had broken his left leg, and his right arm was riddled with stitches. He had no idea how long he'd been there at the hospital or where his wife was.

"Where's Sydney, and how long have I been out," asked Gabriel, trying to position himself in a somewhat comfortable position. He began feeling uneasy. Gabriel knew something was profoundly wrong. He asked the doctor, "Besides the obvious, what did happen? All I remember is screeching tires; it's all a haze after that."

"You've suffered a very brutal concussion, and you've been out for about two days, Mr. Liden. As for your wife, that's a little more complicated," said Dr. Wallace sitting on the edge of his bed. "Your wife has suffered extensive damage to her body, multiple broken bones, and a massive head injury. She's been out ever since she got here."

"What exactly does that mean, Dr. Wallace," asked Gabriel, now nervously trying to get comfortable in the bed.

"Your wife is on life support systems as of two days ago. She is in a coma. We don't know much right now, but it's possible she may never wake. You need to prepare yourself for the worst, Mr. Liden," said Doctor Wallace, grabbing Gabriel's left arm.

"What do you mean, never wake," asked Gabriel?

"There's a distinct possibility, Mr. Liden, that due to her injuries, the severity, that she may either be on life support systems for the rest of her life or if we have to unplug her support systems and her own system may fail."

"I need to see her, please."

Gabriel tried to move from the bed to the cold floor but was stopped by the nurses. They told him, for now, he needed some rest. Now that he was out of critical care. Gabriel could start preparing for when Sydney would awake. He would be healthy, he must, he thought. He could be moved in the morning to a downstairs room in hopes of being discharged. They gave him a mild sedative and something for the pain. Gabriel fell into an uneasy slumber.

While Gabriel was sleeping, they moved him to a room downstairs and began preparing him for his discharge. He woke every once and a while in his new room, but the pain medication kept him sedated. The doctors had been giving him some anxiety medication to help him sleep, and to ease his worry about his wife. The time came when the medicines were stopped, and Gabriel was to wake and begin his road to recovery. Two days had passed since he spoke with Dr. Wallace and his induced easing began, now came the hard part. Gabriel woke once again in a haze and saw a nurse's face. He said, "Do I get to see my wife today?"

The nurse looked at him and told him someone would be coming to visit him in a few minutes. He sat up, trying once again to get comfortable, and called for a nurse to get him some water. One appeared in a moment with a fresh glass of water, and Gabriel drank almost frantically, spilling some on his gown, and a certain paranoia set in. Who's coming to see me? Why haven't they let me see my wife? Suddenly, through the door, a man appeared dressed rather casually. He said,

"Mr. Liden, my name is Mr. Hugh, and I'm a psychologist. I specialize in grief counseling. Sometimes, in circumstances like yours, we try and help people through the process of dealing with a loved one who is in a situation like yours."

"Are you going to take me to see her, I need to see her," said Gabriel trying to get out of bed.

"Mr. Liden, what you want to see is not an easy thing to see. Emotions will be running high, and you will probably feel very overwhelmed. I've dealt with cases like this many times before," said Mr. Hugh.

"Just give me some crutches and we'll go, please," said Gabriel, almost begging the man.

"Please, Mr. Liden, I have a wheelchair just outside the door. I'd like to take you up myself," said Mr. Hugh walking to the entrance of the room and retrieving the chair. He brought it into the room and placed it next to Gabriel's bed. Gabriel pulled himself off the bed and into the chair. Gabriel said, "I'm ready to go now."

Mr. Hugh turned the chair around and began making his way out the door. They went down the hall to the elevator and got in. Mr. Hugh said, "Your loved one is in a state of distress though she will not answer you. Studies have shown that talking to loved ones in these states can help. However, results are not always guaranteed."

The elevator arrived at the tenth floor, and they proceeded left out of the elevator to the nurse's stand. Mr. Hugh made a joke with one of the nurses and said, "We're here to see Mrs. Liden."

The nurse grabbed a chart and began leading them down the hall, Gabriel wheeled by Mr. Hugh. They rounded one corner and stopped at one of the doors.

"Brace yourself, Mr. Liden. This may be difficult," said Mr. Hugh.

They opened the door giving Gabriel a skewed glance of a body motionless in a bed.

"Sydney? Wheel me in," said Gabriel.

Mr. Hugh wheeled him inside. Gabriel got a full view of his wife, bruised, still swollen, fitted with countless instruments keeping her alive. He began feeling ill. He started feeling a dark cloud over him. "Push me closer," said Gabriel reaching for his wife's hand. Mr. Hugh pushed him next to the bed, and he began to tear and cry. "Love, this is all my fault. If we hadn't gone to that place, this would have never happened. Maybe you can hear me, maybe you can't, but I love you, and I will never leave your side." Gabriel cried aloud as he wept with her hand to his mouth, kissing it with tears of pain and guilt.

"Mr. Liden, there is a possibility that she may never come out of this. Perhaps you and I could work on some of these emotions. You are checking out today. You're going to try and resume your life as normally as possible," said Mr. Hugh.

"I'll come every day until she wakes. She will I know it," said Gabriel, wiping the tears from his eyes. "Can you give us a moment, please, Mr. Hugh?"

"Of course, Mr. Liden,"

Mr. Hugh left the room, leaving Gabriel to have some quiet thoughts with his wife. He stood even though it was painful, and he sat on the edge of the bed. He looked at all the tubes coming from the various places in her body, and he began to understand the grave possibility that could be ahead. He started thinking of all the beautiful times they had had over the past while and that he simply could not live without her. He put himself on the edge of the bed and began caressing her bruised arm, being careful of the tube in her hand, and said, "I'm nothing without you, please come back to me, love. I'm going to be here when you wake. We're going to spend the rest of our lives together, and I'll never let anything happen to you again.I promise. I'm going to go now, love, but I'll be back tomorrow and the next day until you walk out that front door with me; I love you. Okay, I'll see you tomorrow. Beautiful Dreams."

Gabriel got off the bed and made his way to Mr. Hugh's room. He told him they could meet once a week, but he'd like to go home for now. Back in his own room on the second floor, Gabriel began gathering his prescriptions and other personal items. Wearing a pair of sweats provided by the hospital, he found his way to the admissions office to sign himself out. The hospital called a cab for him as he made his way to the front of the hospital and waited. His armpits already hurt from the crutches, but he would get used to it. Finally, he got in the cab, and was on the way home. Gabriel's heart felt empty, his head felt heavy, and his leg was in pain. He didn't know what to do.

He made it home just after dark, sat in that old comfy chair, and sank into a deep depression once more. He thought this whole situation was his fault somehow. He took his pain pills and an anxiety pill to ease his thoughts. He eventually became tired and fell into a restless sleep. He tossed and turned until daylight, got up, and eventually got dressed. He called a cab which got him to the hospital just as visiting hours began. He sat there all day, just hoping for her to open her eyes. He begged in silence to see a movement of her arm or even a twitch of a finger, but none occurred. Finally, Mr. Hugh came in halfway through the day and told him to hang on to his faith, and they would see each other the next day. For the most part, the day was long and hard. Eventually, a nurse came in and told him that visiting hours were now over. He kissed his wife's hand, grabbed his crutches, and headed out the door.

Gabriel hailed a cab, but instead of going home, he went to a pub in the midtown district for a drink. He had one, two, three, and a fourth, and he suddenly found himself very intoxicated. He asked the barkeep to call a cab for him. When it arrived, he tried to get up from the seat and use his crutches, but his balance was not to be found. He went straight to the floor. Several people rushed to help him, but his pride began shining at the wrong moment, and he shooed them all away. He began crying and crawling towards the door, eventually realizing he simply couldn't do it himself. A young man helped him to his feet, balanced him on his crutches and got him to the cab. Together they rode to his home on Virginia and Commons. When they arrived, the young man asked the cab to wait as he helped Gabriel up the stairs to his home, and inside to safety. Left alone to sleep off his inebriated state, Gabriel passed out crying in his big comfy chair. The young man took the cab back to the bar paid the tab and enjoyed a drink, compliments of the barkeep.

The night passed with Gabriel in his chair. He greeted the morning with a headache, a feeling of dehydration and a sense he had made a fool of himself. He remembered falling at the bar, but nothing else. How did he get home? How did he get to the chair? He did remember that he had to be at the hospital to meet with Mr. Hugh and sit with his wife. It dawned on him that he had not touched base with work since he left for the weekend trip home. He made a call to his superior at the magazine, letting him know he was alright and what had happened. In lieu of circumstances, he told them he would be taking a week or two off to get his affairs in order and spend some time with Sydney. He dressed, popped two pills for the headache, and drank some water to ease the thirst. He called a cab and made his way to the hospital just as visiting hours began.

His appointment with Mr. Hugh was at one, which left him plenty of time to talk with Sydney. He got to the room as the nurse, who was expecting him, pulled a chair beside her bed. Gabriel began reading to Sydney, a book she had started but not finished before the accident. He felt that hearing the book would comfort her in some way. Reaching up now and again, Gabriel kissed her pale skin, sometimes dropping a tear to roll down her cheek. He was sure that it would only be a matter of days until she woke and was determined to be the first person she saw when her eyes opened. He looked at his watch, and it was five until one, so he headed to the fifth floor to meet Mr. Hugh. He reached his office, and the two greeted each other.

"How are things going, Mr. Liden," said Mr. Hugh.

"Please call me Gabriel. I believe it would make me more comfortable," said Gabriel, sitting in one of the chairs in his office. "Mr. Hugh?"

"Please call me John. Perhaps it would make you feel even more comfortable to call me that," said Mr. Hugh. "How are you, Gabriel?"

"I'm okay," said Gabriel with a barren look on his face.

"A classic answer, Gabriel. Now, I'm going to ask you again. How do you feel?"

"I feel cheated. I feel a lot of my life I've been cheated, one way or another, then something like this happens, and I'm angry," said Gabriel.

"What were you doing out in the outer parts anyway? That's where you were, wasn't it?"

Gabriel began telling Albert the short version of why he was in the outer parts. He spoke of how his father had insulted him for the last time, and that was why they were where they were at the time of the accident. He also told him of how he went to the bar, and the drink seemed to make it go away. John warned him that that type of coping would get him nowhere and asked him to turn to his faith if he had any. They talked for the remainder of the time allotted.

In the last few minutes of the appointment, John leaned forward and their gazes locked. In those moments, he reminded Gabriel that it would be better if he allowed himself to consider the worst-case scenario. What would he do if the bills kept piling and he couldn't pay them anymore? But, Gabriel told him he wasn't going to think about that because he was sure Sydney was going to wake up.

He left the office and went back to the tenth floor to be with Sydney. He stayed for the remainder of the day, lamenting over the situation, crying ever so often, talking ever so sweetly. Once again, the nurse came in and told him visiting hours were over. He kissed his love ever so gently, made his way to the exit of the building, and caught a cab. This time instead of making a fool of himself, he made a stop along the way home to the liquor store and grabbed a bottle of whiskey. It was dark when he arrived at his home. He went to his big comfy chair after he grabbed a glass and poured himself a drink. He felt the first drink warm him and the second start to change his thoughts a little. By the fourth, he was uncontrollably crying into his glass. He knew he was getting his feelings out, but he would not remember in the morning, so it was for the better.

He passed out around eleven, his glass spilling to the floor, the bottle almost empty.

The next week went by very slowly, and the bottles kept mounting. Gabriel was not holding fast in his faith but placing his faith in escaping. He went to the meeting with John that week. All Gabriel heard was preparation for the worst, not jubilant expectation for the waking of his love. Once again, John warned him of his drinking. He pleaded with him not to go down that road. John suggested that he go back to work and try to focus on something besides the current, apparent distraction. Gabriel said he would give it a try. He went back to Sydney's room and stayed for the rest of the day. When the nurse came in, he knew it was time to go home. As he always did, he made it to the liquor store and purchased his ticket to escape for the night.

The night went as planned, crying, yelling, and lamenting, but when he woke, he remembered what John had said about work. Every morning he woke, he felt worse and worse, so Gabriel, seeing the signs of destruction, called his superior at the magazine and asked if he could work half days the coming week. His boss was happy to hear that he wanted to try and get back in the game, so to speak. He went to the hospital for the next few days, going lightly on the drinking, preparing his mind for stimulation, rather than sorrow.

The next week came, and he woke early to get a jump on the day. He arrived at nine o'clock sharp and sat in his desk chair after a long absence trying to catch up with the new material. Everyone dropped by his desk and told him all would be well, and that he and Sydney were in their prayers. He found that it was not easy to concentrate on work. He only thought of Sydney.

The midday came, and Gabriel was happy to go and see his love, but he knew that once he arrived, sorrow and grief would take over. He arrived around one and said hello to the nurses that he knew so well. Today, they would do a crossword puzzle together. He would get ideas from her and then fill in the answers she wished. When one finds tragedy, one finds way to survive.

Gabriel still thought that at any moment, she might wake. He wanted to be there, so he went back every day for the next two months, until one day he arrived home receiving a certified letter in the mail. Gabriel opened it and read it. It told him of a living will that the insurance company was aware of, that he was not. In the living will, if Sydney were to ever be placed on life support systems, and did not wake after three months, they were to stop the support systems and try to let her survive on her own. The will would let her body pass on if she did not wake. Gabriel was outraged.

He immediately went to the phone, for he knew the three-month mark was in a couple of days. He dialed the insurance company's number and was placed with a representative. The representative went over the clause of the living will, of which they were concerned. They told and retold Gabriel there was nothing he could do about it legally, those were her wishes. Gabriel was determined not to give up. He called the law firm, but it was after hours, so he did what he had been doing for the last two months and reached for the bottle. He called after a few drinks and left John a message. He didn't know what to do. He drank himself into oblivion. He remembered to set the alarm for eight so he could call the law firm. He sat in his comfy chair, his hands now tied. He eventually slipped off into drunken sleep. Goodnight, Gabriel.

Morning arose, and a blaring alarm went off at eight o'clock sharp. Gabriel was startled and began getting ready for work then remembered why he set the alarm. He called the law firm, and the receptionist answered,

"Hello, Maslow and Dietz."

"I need to speak to the Senior Partner about my wife's living will," said Gabriel feeling a raging hangover.

"Mr. Maslow deals with most of those matters, I'll transfer you," said the receptionist.

A beeping noise began and went on for a minute or two until finally, a voice came on the line.

"This is Mr. Maslow. How can I help you?"

"Mr. Maslow, I received a certified letter about my wife's living will who is in a coma," said Gabriel calmly. "Certainly, there's been some mistake with the clause in question."

"I assume you're speaking of Sydney Bloomfield. I was contacted by the insurance agency last week."

"Well, actually, it's Sydney Liden now, Mr. Maslow," said Gabriel. "Surely you don't mean they're going to pull the plug on my wife in a couple of days."

"Mr. Liden, this is a prevalent thing, spouses make living wills sometimes years before they marry and spouses don't know about them, but the insurance company always does. They're always out to cut costs. In this case, when Mrs. Bloomfield, I'm sorry, Mrs. Liden, came to me a few years after her mother or father had just died, and she made these arrangements. I'd like to tell you there's something I can do for you, but these were your wife's wishes."

"So, you're telling me, in two days, the insurance company is going to pull the plug," said Gabriel near tears. "There's nothing I can do?"

"I'm sorry, Mr. Liden. My advice to you is to go love your wife and hope for the best. I have a call I need to take, Mr. Liden. So, I hope the best for you, Mr. Liden, and your wife as well. I will bid you a good day."

Gabriel hung up the phone, called his boss, and told him he would be out for the next few days. He went immediately to the hospital and into John's office, but he was not there. He went to the office of the hospital administrator, introduced himself, and pleaded his case. Once again, he was told the same thing; you cannot go against the living will. She made these choices and they must be honored. Exhausted, Gabriel went to be by his wife's side. He cried. He asked her why she would take this choice away from him. Why had she not told him? He was enraged, but there was nothing he could do. He stayed the remainder of the day by his wife's side. He knew tomorrow they would pull the plug on her life. He waited for the nurse to come in and tell him it was time to go, and eventually, she did. He kissed her arm and began crying as he left the room. He looked back but knew he would only see her for a little while tomorrow. He caught a cab home and began crying into his glass as he sat in his big comfy chair. He cried himself dry and set the alarm to wake in the morning. He made his way across the room to get his blanket, and fell into sleep. Sweet dreams Gabriel...

Chapter 14

The Keeper

The alarm sounded at six. Gabriel wanted to get an early start to the day. He made a steaming hot cup of coffee and began preparing himself. His heart felt dark. He felt empty. He was lost, but he knew that he had to face the coming day. He showered and dressed in his best suit and called a cab. The cab arrived in a few minutes, and he was on his way. He stopped to get her flowers, for he knew she would like them.

He arrived around eight and climbed the stairs rather than using the elevator to her tenth-floor room. The early morning quiet in her room was disturbed by the beeping of the heart monitor and the sighing of the ventilator that breathed for her over the past few days. Occasional sounds from the nurses' station in the hall outside reminded him that others would soon take control of his life and of Sydney's.

Gabriel took Sydney's hand. He whispered his love to her in a million different ways; a million different times; he felt he could not say it enough, or with the heart he meant her to feel. The moments slipped into hours and the hours passed until the clock on the wall proclaimed it was 5 o'clock on the last day of their life together.

He began to feel sick. He wanted to run. He could not stand the pain. He knew she was going to die and there was no way to stop them from taking her away. He took one last look at her frail body and sprinted out of the hospital. He took a cab home and sank into his deep dark suicidal depression. He still had pain pills from his leg injury and he gripped them in his hands. I will join her, he thought. He grabbed his bottle of whiskey and began drinking. "This was not a cry for help, but a need to crossover," Gabriel cried, "the keeper would understand." He drank for an hour, slouching in his comfy chair, clutching the pills just waiting for the call saying she was gone. He cried in panic. He cried in fear, but eventually, he cried himself to sleep.

He was caught in the clutches of nightmares when the ring of his phone broke through the haze that was his mind. He grabbed his crutches and made it to the kitchen clumsily to answer the phone.

"Hello," said Gabriel with his stomach in his throat.

"Gabriel, it's John. You're never going to believe this, are you alright," he asked?

"Look, just tell me it's over so I can get this over with," said Gabriel, still holding himself up, drunk and sleepy.

"Gabriel, she woke up. Come down to the hospital, come on, man," said John excitedly. Gabriel had a moment of disbelief. He clutched the phone and prayed he was not still dreaming.

"Look, I've had a few drinks. Can you repeat that I'm not sure I heard you? Did you say she woke up?"

"Yes, get down here, Gabriel," said John.

Gabriel had already hung up the phone and was dialing a cab. The wait for the cab seemed to take forever, but eventually, it arrived. He hobbled down the stairs screaming to the driver, "Metropolis Mercy Hospital, and fast!!!"

He arrived at the hospital a short time later. An orderly waited for him with a wheelchair to take him quickly to his wife. The elevator door opened. The orderly pushed him in. They pushed the button for the tenth floor, and it began moving. The bell rang for each floor: seven, eight, nine, ding-ten, and they were off down the hall to her room. When he reached the door, he saw her there with a crowd of doctors around her.

"It's a miracle, Gabriel," said one of the nurses whom he had known for the last three months.

He wheeled himself in. He cried, "Sydney, love, move, out of my way!" The doctors made a pathway for his wheelchair, and he made it to the side of the bed. Sydney's eyes were open, but she was still laying down. He grabbed her hand, and she squeezed, but she was weak. One of the doctors chimed in,

"Her muscles have atrophied a bit. She hasn't used them for months; that is why she seems weak, Mr. Liden."

"So, she needs physical therapy, let's get started," said Gabriel crying in joy.

"Mr. Liden, we've got to keep her awake and stable for a while before we can start such things," said the doctor through a smile that was shared by all the staff.

"Gabriel, come closer," said Sydney very softly. "They say I've been out three months, but you were here every day, thank you. I love you, Gabe. We got through this; we can get through anything."

The doctors moved in front of Gabriel and told him that they needed to run some tests. He should go home and come back in the morning. He kissed his love and was wheeled out of the room and back to the elevator. Gabriel was supposed to have his cast off in three days, but he went down to the emergency room and asked to have it removed that day. They took some x-rays and found that the pin in his leg was placed well, and the bones had healed well enough. They removed it in the emergency room. He was then free of that burden, the burden of the loss of his wife, and the physical hindrance of his leg. In his mind, the ordeal was over, and it was. Gabriel showed up the next morning for therapy and the next, and the next time, until the time when she was healthy again. They moved through those days, living together, progressing as one. However, it would be a few months until Sydney and Gabriel were back to work and feeling like themselves. Sydney's wounds healed, but the pin in Gabriel's leg was something of a nuisance at first. He knew he had to get back on his new Gavali, and his wife on hers as well.

Spring was in the air, and they had both lived through the tragedy and come out on the other side. Their love was unmatched in all of my stories, but I did promise you a love story, and I guess you should know how it ends. The two enjoyed their bicycle rides and their food. They even indulged in a bit of wine now and then. However, Gabriel never touched whiskey again. Time flew by for the couple, a lot of ups, and as most, some downs. One year turned to two, then two to ten, and then ten to twenty. Their thirtieth-anniversary celebration was that trip to the far seas metropolis. They chose not to have children, or rather Sydney had been rendered unable to have children due to the accident, but they lived and loved.

Tragically, Sydney going for a regular check-up at the age of fifty-nine discovered she was in a latent stage of breast cancer, a fate her mother had known much too early in her life. She went through chemotherapy, battled, and put up a fight, but her body was ready to pass over. On beautiful summer's morning, she died in the comfort of her lover's arms and was buried just a few days later, Gabriel giving the eulogy. Gabriel, in the end, took it well for he thought he had lost her years before, and to have had her as long as he had felt like a blessing. Gabriel retired from the magazine and took up a position at the Highland Boys School as the socialization teacher taking a few scholarship students under his belt. Now, my friends, a love story may not always end in a tragedy or tell such great truths, but Gabriel's time is near, so perhaps we should check in with him. Gabriel sat at his desk during what he thought to be a normal day. Suddenly a voice saying, "Gabriel, can you hear me," rang in his head. He was startled at first, but the voice persisted, "Gabriel, it is your time; the keeper is calling."

Gabriel began to get a little scared as he felt his chest begin to palpitate. Finally, Gabriel called out, "I am ready to join my wife."

"You will feel no pain Gabriel, call no one. Now is your time." Gabriel sat in his chair in his office and began spiraling out of his body. He did not worry. You will wake in a moment, Gabriel. Just relax...

Chapter 15

A Final Chapter

Gabriel woke to a very bright, serene light, one he seemed to recognize somehow. He was comforted and calm. He soon found himself standing in the middle of a large white room with no one around him. No angels, no gates, no holy choirs, he began to wonder. He stood motionless for a moment, bewildered, and said, "Hello, is there anyone there," but no one answered. "Is this what the great secret holds, brilliant white light and utter silence? Is this what has been kept for me? Can someone tell me where my wife is? Can you please tell me where my wife is?"

Suddenly, off in the distance, a figure seemed to be approaching. Gabriel did not recognize this person, and he asked as the man approached, "Who are you, and where am I?"

The figure came closer and became clearer. He was a dashing young man, well dressed and well-groomed. He looked at Gabriel and said, "It's good to see you, Gabriel. How are you?"

"Do we know each other? I'm very confused. I left my body at the school only to end up here in this place. Are you the keeper?" asked Gabriel.

"I am "a" keeper, Gabriel, of a place, the place you are in," said the man.

"What is this place? Is this heaven?" asked Gabriel curiously. "I need to know something. Where is my wife? Can you tell me where she is?"

"Gabriel, this is where you always get confused. This is not heaven, nor is this hell. This is a place for people who tried to do the right thing, but things may not have worked out as they had planned," said the man.

"What do you mean may not have worked out as they planned? Are you telling me my life did not go the way I wanted? My life was wonderful. I was truthful. I lived. I loved, isn't that what the keeper wants for us all?" he asked, not understanding the man's sentiment.

"Gabriel, I believe you are missing the point here. You shouldn't really be asking yourself what this place is. Ask instead why you are in this place. You always get confused here," said the man.

"I'm not sure what you mean by I always get confused here, but okay. Why am I here then?"

"You're here because the High keeper knows you did the best you could, you tried your best, but you broke a cardinal rule for which he made an exception." said the man.

"What cardinal rule?" he asked.

"You took your own life," said the man.

Suddenly, Gabriel began having flashes of images. Images of his life flashed by he did not remember. He began seeing himself in the comfy chair, a bottle of whiskey, and a bottle of pills strewn on the floor. Gabriel said, "These are not the images of my life, dear keeper."

"These are the images you blocked out. See, every time you get here, you get confused. You say you don't remember that part of your life, when in fact, that was the last moment of your life. The rest is always a lie. Remember that phone call from the hospital, the one where Sydney awakened?"

"Yes, but what does that have to do with anything? How was any of my life a lie?" asked Gabriel?

"Well, she didn't wake Gabriel. You've just suppressed that fact over so many, many, many cycles. It's amazing how you forget every time," said the man. "We've been over this well over a hundred times; your life ended that night. You make up the rest as each turn comes."

"Where's my wife?" asked Gabriel in a demanding voice.

"Your wife is with the High keeper," said the man.

"Take me to her now," said Gabriel, demanding once again.

"Gabriel, the time for demands was, oh a thousand years ago. That's about how long you've been cycling through these lies," said the man. "See Gabriel, The High keeper was merciful on you instead of sending you to the other place. He sent you here because you took your own life. After all, you wanted to be with her. A suicide of love is partially pardonable."

"I didn't take my life. I was just with her a few years ago. I don't understand what you're saying. Tell me this is not true. Please take me to my wife."

"I cannot do that. Just think about it, Gabriel. She died just like her mother. It was the easiest way you knew how to let her go. It was the easiest way she would have wanted to go. You have a choice every time you show up here, again, again, and again. You can stay with us or cycle again and create a life, half of it facts, and half of it lies. The original mistake that plagued you while in the metropolis is the same choice posed to you here, and every time you choose to cycle again," said the man. "There is someone here who wants to show you around this place, but you keep choosing to cycle back to lies. In that respect, you get to replay your life as you would have really wanted it to end, not in a chair with a stomach full of pills and whiskey."

"Who wants to show me around," asked Gabriel?

Suddenly, James Liden appeared from off in the distance walking towards the two men, and Gabriel began to get furious. The man said, "Remember this a place for those who tried to do the right thing, but things may not have turned out the way they wanted them to."

"Come with me, son. We'll finally get to know one another," said a young James Liden.

Gabriel began to feel sick, "You mean, I will never truly see my wife again, and you want me to let him show me around this hell for eternity. Is this how it is every time? Are these my only choices? I would rather choose a false life than eternity with him. Is this not hell?"

"No, this is a good place, Gabriel. You're going to have to make the same choice over and over again, just as you've done in the past. We just wish you'd change your mind," said the man.

"I want no more of this, put me back. I want to cycle again," said Gabriel falling to his knees.

"So then, just to make sure, tell me, and we'll start again. Or we'll start anew, which is it?"

"I'll cycle again," said Gabriel closing his eyes and wishing for death.

"Gabriel, just as long as you know it's not real. You do this every time, when will you learn," said the man.

"Please come with me, Gabriel," said James pleading with his son.

"I want to cycle," Gabriel pleaded.

"Very well, we'll see you in a while. You'll just be left with the same choice over and over again for all eternity," said the man.

"Then, I'll cycle for eternity..."

"Very well, then Gabriel, sleep..."

In the city, there is the hustle and bustle day and night. There are those that need the light, and then there are those that feed off the darkness of the night. Some run to keep in shape. Some never leave the confines of their shelter. Some do not have shelter, and some enjoy food while others go without. Cities, including this one, are a combination of grand and seedy. The rich get richer while the poor grow poorer, but the middle never changes.

Gabriel, perhaps a wish ...

The End of The Beginning of The Cycle

MEET THE AUTHOR

A.W. Stripling Jr. currently resides in Portland, Oregon with his German Shepherd Gracie. He holds a degree in Psychology from Ole Miss and enjoys interacting with people in whatever way possible. When he is not writing, you will often see him walking the streets of Portland listening to music and enjoying a coffee beverage from his favorite coffee shop. He dabbles in electronics and loves brainstorming about things like marketing, autonomous vehicles, and the exploration of the human mind. Most evenings are spent editing and writing notes for new books. He currently works with his family and their COVID-Era launched non-profit, iNSL.org, helping children learn about STEM using auto racing as a virtual platform.

www.ingramcontent.com/pod-product-compliance
Lightning Source LLC
Chambersburg PA
CBHW030426310726
48979CB00009B/1632/J

* 9 7 8 1 9 4 2 3 5 7 8 0 3 *